the CANDLE MAKER

the
CANDLE
MAKER

A NOVEL

JAMES RYAN ORR

New York

the CANDLE MAKER
A NOVEL

This is a work of fiction. Names, characters, businesses, places, events, and incidents are either the products of the author's imagination or used in a fictitious manner. Any resemblance to actual persons, living or dead, or actual events is purely coincidental.

Published in New York, New York, by Morgan James Publishing. Morgan James and The Entrepreneurial Publisher are trademarks of Morgan James, LLC. www.MorganJamesPublishing.com

The Morgan James Speakers Group can bring authors to your live event. For more information or to book an event visit The Morgan James Speakers Group at www.TheMorganJamesSpeakersGroup.com.

Shelfie

A **free** eBook edition is available
with the purchase of this print book.

CLEARLY PRINT YOUR NAME ABOVE IN UPPER CASE

Instructions to claim your free eBook edition:
1. Download the Shelfie app for Android or iOS
2. Write your name in **UPPER CASE** above
3. Use the Shelfie app to submit a photo
4. Download your eBook to any device

ISBN 978-1-63047-969-5 paperback
ISBN 978-1-63047-970-1 eBook
ISBN 978-1-63047-971-8 hardcover
Library of Congress Control Number:
2016901834

Cover Design by:
Megan James

Interior Design by:
Bonnie Bushman
The Whole Caboodle Graphic Design

In an effort to support local communities and raise awareness and funds, Morgan James Publishing donates a percentage of all book sales for the life of each book to Habitat for Humanity Peninsula and Greater Williamsburg

Get involved today, visit
www.MorganJamesBuilds.com

To my wife and our daughters,
who taught me how to look for the light in others
and brought me that much closer to the Candle Maker.

Also, special thanks to Michael Crum
for the seed, the sun, and the water.

The Candle Maker gifts a portion to us,
To each of us, a shimmering shard of a much greater heart
placed lovingly within.

Is it given for us to guard and protect,
or is it given to guide and direct?

Contents

Prologue

Candle

All of his life Phillip believed that there was a real, tangible, pick-it-up-and-hold-it candle within his chest. This candle, lit, glowing, and working its light through him, was something that took him years to fully come to terms with. To say that a belief like this was easy to accept is to say only a fraction of the truth. At times Phillip struggled greatly with it. To allow himself completely over to such a notion—the burning, the light spreading into his dreams, his interactions, his mistakes, his pain, his triumphs—was something he had to grow into, like stepping into the worn brown dress shoes left behind in his father's closet. In time it would all fit. In time he would grow into the wingspan of the light that he held within. In time he would find himself beyond the doubt and into the resolute knowledge, carving notion into stone, that there was indeed a candle, lit and glowing, in the middle of his chest, right where the heart resides.

It was evident early on in his life that he held an affinity toward light, an uncanny draw and pull toward it, especially the warm, welcoming, and quiet type produced by candles. His mother Tabitha, in her best summation of the relationship that was shared between Phillip and candlelight, described it to herself (for motherly assurance) as a level of friendship. She thought often, long and searchingly, of this so called "friendship" that was displayed by her beautiful baby boy. It was something she wrestled with, swaying in her thoughts, a pendulum of decision, then indecision, swinging into the good of it all and then into the slopes of uncertainty and worry of there being something wrong with her son. *How many kids consider light to be their friend?* she often thought. *On the other side, how many kids should be so lucky?* Ultimately she understood.

The best displays of the swinging that Tabitha thought, felt, and lived with concerning this "friendship" are found within her journal. Page after page, the chronicling of the ever-expanding world of her precious child, the journal was her way to attempt at capturing the connecting days, each a milestone to be noted, each a fresh discovery of a new life and an older life permitted to witness new life over again. It is within her journal that Tabitha noted on more than one occasion the fascination that light held over Phillip.

Journal Entry

"Today I tried feeding Phillip mashed carrots for the first time. I say tried because by the stains on my dress and his little shirt, I am not altogether sure about the success of it. He squinted and mashed his eyes shut as if I had fed him a spoonful of mustard. He is one silly boy…and the faces he makes. He actually ended up with some smeared behind his left ear. How is such a thing even possible? How do carrots end up behind someone's ear? He was also gurgling and making all types of noises trying to talk to me. I wonder how he sees things around him. I wonder what is going on behind that little face. I can hardly wait for him to start speaking, letting me in on his world. Also, I lit one of the kitchen candles and he started sputtering out sounds, spitting out all sorts of gibberish, drooling and grinning the whole time. He even started giggling at one point. He certainly seems to like candles, my little orange-eared, babbling moth. I wish Eric were here to see this little miracle in our kitchen."

Later on in the life of a growing Phillip, his mother growing right along with him, a pinchful of journal pages later, another occurrence….

Journal Entry

"Candle, or as Phillip pronounces it, Can-dol (slow on the "Can" and very quick with the "dol")," is his first word. I talk to him all the day long and I am guessing that I must talk about candles quite a bit. To say that I am proud of my little guy is an understatement. He's begun to speak to me, let me in on his world, and the very first thing that he wants to talk about is

light. I am moved daily by his joy, and I can't help but feel like he holds something special inside him. It's quite astonishing, the whole idea of raising a life. Becoming a mother is a beautiful thing, and I have been blessed with a remarkable son to share this journey with."

Further along into her journal....

Journal Entry

"Today—how can I put this correctly— Phillip did something that struck me as…as odd. Today he was pointing up to one of the kitchen candles, the one on the table, and then he was pointing back to his chest. He did this repeatedly while I secretively watched him, playing that I was more occupied with laundry sorting. I admit I was curiously spying on him, quite baffled by his behavior. Then he noticed me, looked right at me, and smiled…pointed to the candle once more, then his little hand back to his chest again, saying "light." He smiled again, this time bigger, then stumbled over to me and gave me a hug. He held on for a few seconds, then tottered over to his blocks, sat down, and started his building with stacking and unstacking. Not entirely sure what to think about this, except I got the feeling that he was saying that there is light inside of him. It was something to think about while finishing up with the clothes, and I suppose that most mothers feel at times that the whole responsibility of motherhood is a bit overwhelming. I know that he is a great boy and that he is very bright; it was just a bit alarming to feel for a moment that he was trying to tell me something so big. "

Phillip continued to grow, inward and outward, ever expanding like an unfolding universe, as did Tabitha's heart with him. There is pristine joy in the watching of something good grow, especially when the person watching has played a part in the creation. Perhaps it is a piece of art, the writing of an emotion-capturing poem, the coming up of flowers planted in a garden, or in its most brilliant form, the giving and nurturing of a life. This was not lost, nor completely found, with Tabitha, as she was close to the very picture of patience, understanding, and loving communion between mother and child. There were times of nerve testing—the occasional broken glass (window and vase) here and there and sharp-cornered toys left to be stepped upon by bare feet in the middle of nights—but all in all, her time with her beautiful and precious boy was dear to her. Who is to know, within the golden symphony played between and within parent and child, who shapes the other more? All of this she pondered as they grew together.

PART
ONE

Chapter 1

A Little Light
Inside a Little Boy

Grass stains, muddy boots, and scraped knees accompanied Phillip's journey, along with the sprinkled moments that reopened, for his mother, the puzzle of light and the effect that it held over him.

"Mom?" Walking up and looking up to her, Phillip repeated, "Mom? Can I tell you something?"

Tabitha looked down, closing the book she was reading, smiling at her little shaggy-haired love. "Of course you can, dear. My ears are wide open and completely at your service." She tried her best to wiggle them but couldn't, so instead she exaggerated her eyes up and down.

"Something serious," he said, through a slightly squinted face. "No joking."

3

"Yes, sweetie," she responded, while intently looking at his knees for scrapes and his boots for mud, half expecting the remnants of some minor, boyish mischief to be about him. "I am listening, no joking around."

"Mom...this may sound a bit weird...never mind, it's really nothing...it's silly." He turned to walk away, but his mother reached and gently turned him back around so his face could be seen.

"Phillip," she addressed him, leaning down so that her eyes could meet his, "if it means something to you, something enough to share, then it means something to me, something enough to listen."

He thought about her eyes now, looking up and into them searchingly, how they seemed to smile at times. With an inward breath, then with a sigh, he let the words out: "Mom," scanning her face, anticipating reaction from what he was about to say, "there is a candle—a real candle—inside of me."

"Well," discretely taking stock of the candles positioned around the kitchen and main room with half a hunch to find one with a bite or two missing, she asked, "does this candle of yours have a particular flavor?"

Phillip's face folded completely at this. "Mom, I didn't eat it...you don't eat candles...I knew this was a bad idea to talk about."

"Okay," Tabitha prodded, now game to this interaction, attentive, "where is this candle of yours....in your feet...in your hair..."and, with emphasis on this last part, "in your belly?"

His head wobbled, air expelled nasally in an innocent frustration. "Mom, I didn't eat any candles…I knew I should have said nothing…I never should of…." He turned to walk away again but was gently corralled once more.

"Okay, all ears now, no joking around, no talk about eating candles, okay?" his mother soothed, wholly attentive now, just naturally flowing within a state that overcomes parents trying their best in moments such as these, a deeply buried, sacred tone they are able to find within them to express to their children a type of sincere empathy, hushing the outside world with a true face and set of eyes, appearing fully, listening completely, within the moment. Tabitha, now delicate but stone strong, continued, "I am sorry Phillip, it's just that I don't really see what you're talking about…I would like to, though. Can you help me understand just exactly what you are trying to say?"

Phillip, under the spell of the sacred tone, let all of his thoughts out: "Mom, I didn't eat any candles, I promise. For so long now I have felt it…I have to tell someone, not just any someone, somebody close…you, I have to tell you. There is a candle, a burning candle inside of me." His hands now moved up to his chest, right where the heart resides.

Phillip felt the weight of secrecy lifted, his mother accepting the burden of her son's cryptic message, her emotions hanging substantially on the word "burning," the whole conversation growing out of an innocent talk into something troubling, yet not alarming, as if her mind had to make a judgment call with no clear stance for either side. Her mind flashed back to the multitude of moments that dotted the path past to present, all the times that Phillip spoke about and seemingly was drawn to light, and now she felt as if she had fallen asleep on her watch over Phillip.

"How long, Phillip," she gently spoke, "how long has it been hurting?"

"Burning, mom, not hurting. It doesn't hurt at all." Nothing on his face suggested that Tabitha read otherwise. "Just a little light inside a little boy."

Working within the judgment call of what was going on with her precious and sweet boy, slightly eased by his response, she delved deeper: "A little light inside a little boy, huh?"

"Yes, mom, just like that."

"No hurting, no pain, Phillip?"

"No pain, mom, just light, warm light, I feel it in there." His little hands again touched his chest.

The spell of the sacred tone lifted as if it had drifted down to chaperone the dance of great truths shared between parent and child, powerful truths that had come up from deep portions to dance on the surface of words, exchange bow and curtsey, and drift away back to the faint edges of mind behind mind, where emotions grow.

Unable to help herself, after a series of pushes, pokes, a great deal of soft prodding near his abdomen and sternum, and, she couldn't resist, a wrist to his forehead, she stood perplexed, firm on the notion of calling for Dr. Jenkins the very next day.

"You're sure that you are fine…no pain?"

His face lifted up from the seriousness and broke into the charming grin that young people naturally carry about them. "Yes, mom, I am fine, nothing wrong at all…I just had to tell you."

He turned, bounced off down the hall, relieved to have shared his secret, and more so to have shared to such a listener, knowing his words found their way into her concern and understanding. She watched down the hall as he skipped, her sweet and precious little boy.

Chapter 2

Drawing
Dr. Jenkins

H e's perfectly fine, there is nothing physically wrong with young Phillip," Dr. Jeremiah Jenkins, a family friend, stated in a soft, yet absent voice, putting his glasses in his coat pocket, rubbing the back of his hand against his chin. "This candle business he has been speaking about, how long has he been going on about it?"

"To be quite honest, and part of my alarm in calling you to see him," she answered, looking over her shoulder at Phillip, sprawled out on the floor, doodling around with his drawing pencils and paper, "for as long as I can remember, off and on since he first started speaking."

"Well," no longer rubbing his chin, the good doctor vacantly stared in the general direction of Phillip, focusing inwardly as was his demeanor, "I have heard of this sort of thing, a condition like this." Sensing how his words may be causing concern outside of his own mind, he added, "Nothing to worry about really, not necessarily a bad type of condition, just a way in which some young children see the world outside of them, and in Phillip's case," glancing down at the intently sketching boy, "the world within them as well."

"Are you sure he is fine? With everything that happened…with all that Eric went through," Tabitha's face and words pleaded for validation and something certain to lean on. "I don't want Phillip to have any troubles…"

The doctor, rubbed his chin again, looking inward, vacantly outward, searching inside. "Yes, the business with Eric was difficult…Tabitha…please know," outward now, faintly smiling, "Phillip is fine, more than fine, in fact. Please, my dear friend, understand that what we are seeing in young Phillip is far from…beyond far from, what we saw Eric walk through. Please do not put another thought in that direction. I have an acquaintance, an old friend, really—her name is Dr. Lynn—who's an exceptional person in this field of study, years devoted to the mind and all of its caverns, and she is scheduled to speak at the University in a few months' time. I shall open a line of correspondence with her on this matter, and I have no doubts that she will gladly meet with us to help shed," his eyes twinkling with his attempt at humor, "some light on our little situation."

Tabitha, now much calmer, allowed the joke to soften her mood enough to invoke a smile. "Okay, if you say he is fine then I will trust in that. Please keep me posted with any news, and we will start making preparations as well. Thank you, Jeremiah."

"More than fine," the doctor replied, now both hands in his pockets, "and I will most definitely keep you up to date with what I gather from Dr. Lynn. I am sure what she will have to say will prove to be helpful. And, Tabitha... you're welcome."

At this, Phillip walked up to Dr. Jenkins, who stood almost twice his height, holding out with both of his little hands, with the tips of his fingers, a sheet of paper. "For you, Dr. Jenkins. I made this for you."

Phillip proudly handed it over. "It's a picture of you—you help people!" and with that he turned and skipped out of the room, radiating the energy that young people carry.

Dr. Jenkins looked down at the drawing in his hands: glasses, beard, overly bushy eyebrows, even the shoes matched up in color. But there in the middle of his chest, where the heart resides, there was a candle, a lit candle, with yellows and soft oranges, in young handmade streaks. There was light glowing out of him.

A smile, the strange, real type, the kind that forms only when deep strings have been strummed, opened across his face, but just for a moment, and then inward he went, into his thinking, before heading out the door to write a letter to Dr. Lynn.

Chapter 3

The Girl in the Green Dress

U p to this point, Phillip held, within his heart of innermost hearts, tightly onto the belief of the candle inside, with its soft glow warmly working, streaking from the inside out. Opening up what is inside to the world around can be a beautiful experience, such as a butterfly that has been tightly tucked into a leathery husk of a cocoon, unfolding, working its wings to freedom. Or, the process of sharing one's real self can be disastrous, swinging wide the gate to all the hallowed places and feelings within, only to be bruised, then deciding that all is cold and to be untrusted, closing up, barricading the door from what might come in and what might go out.

Phillip stood in front of his class, about to share a beginning-of-the-year writing assignment, an introductory piece about who he is and what is important to him.

He held firmly to the paper, looking down at what was written, glancing up over the top edge of the paper at the class. His teacher, smiling, in the back of the room with her arms casually folded, encouraged him: "Whenever you're ready Phillip; you are going to do great."

Through a bit of nerves, clearing his throat, he began, "I am Phillip. I live only a short distance away from school, and soon I will be walking to school and home by myself. My mom wants to walk with me for a few days just to make sure I know the way." Another clearing of his voice, looking around at his classmates, then Phillip blurted, "I don't know my father."

Snickering erupted from a group of boys in the back corner, which to the teacher's credit was quickly smashed under a severe glare in their direction, but which softened back upon Phillip to carry on.

"But I do know my mom, and she is the most amazing person I have ever met. She is strong, funny, loving, and a great listener. She always encourages me to do my best. I like to build things. I enjoy reading and writing. Also, I am very fond of drawing pictures."

Phillip then turned his paper over in his hands, around for everyone to see, handing a piece of himself over to the class. It was a portrait of him, carefully detailed, with shaggy dark hair, worn sneakers, and right in the middle of his chest, where the heart resides, a candle complete with flame.

Phillip had gone this far, so he finished by explaining, "There I am, with a candle inside."

At this the boys of the back corner fully exploded with snide, loud laughter, which once again, to the teacher's credit, was pummeled beneath a stare and face that could cut an apple, along with a strongly darted statement: "It is obvious that there are those in my class that are too immature for listening and sharing. Perhaps a word home to the parents of these few about the necessity of respect and class etiquette is in order." Turning her harsh glare from the boys of the back corner, softening, softening more, back to Phillip, her face and words spoke gently now: "Thank you, Phillip, for sharing. It is clear that you do have a way with words, and I agree with your mother—you do have great talent at drawing."

In this moment, Phillip couldn't quite believe his eyes, but as she was speaking to him, he thought he could see, just for a brief glimmer of a second, a lit candle within his teacher's chest. It flickered and was gone before he could believe or not believe.

"Well done, Phillip. Could you please place your paper on my desk and have a seat."

———⊗⊗⊗———

Later, at recess, the boys of the back corner caught up with Phillip, and amidst the delighted squeals and far-carrying laughter that accompanies trees, sand, and a field of play, their hurtful words were hidden, camouflaged within the concert of noise.

"A candle…of all the stupid things I have heard in my time, a blooming candle. What kind of fool goes about thinking he's got a candle inside of him?" this coming from the obvious ringleader of the group.

Another chimed in mockingly, "Yeah…his mother loves him so much though…so loving and caring. Perhaps old dear mother should take her son to get his head checked for bats flying around."

The last of the three now, chomping at the bit to outdo his pals, threw the biggest verbal stone: "No wonder your father is gone…he left because his dear old son is soft in the head."

Phillip, now tense and more than ever in his life wanting to harden his hand and swing it, was stopped in his tracks by a voice, a rather jarring voice.

"Excuse me." All turned to see a dainty girl with long brown hair and wearing a green dress. "I hope you know that right now the three of you," she addressed the boys of the back corner coolly, "look mighty tough picking on one kid."

Her tone shifted from cool to very much heated. "Well, now I am here and the odds," she threatened, eyeing each of them in sequence, "have changed quite a bit."

Although she looked small for her age, the girl's words and posture held a certain command. Boldly staring at the three, she issued her challenge: "If you're so tough, I am going to want to see just how tough the three of you are. Say one more word… I don't mind getting my dress dirty today."

The three boys of the back corner clenched their lips, each looking to one another for the word or nod to continue their assault, but it didn't come. Something about this girl, as they were each individually starting to realize they had never met before, was off-putting and, strangely, although she was small for her age, powerful.

"Just who are you anyway?" asked the obvious ringleader, knowing he had to play for his followers, but not play too hard or else the little girl might just get her dress dirty.

She eyed him as if he were made of wet paper. "Names aren't so important, not as important as words or actions, especially actions—they mean the world. And I see by your lack thereof that you are just a group of cowards."

Stone-eyeing them even more heatedly, one by one by one, face to face to face, the girl continued flexing her fingers open and closed into fists. "I suggest you boys move along," pausing a moment for effect to look down at her hand tightening and loosening, "before I start acting."

The ringleader, realizing how badly he was losing face, tried desperately to save it. "Come on, guys. We don't need to waste our time messing with these two." Turning and being followed by the other two, he led them off into the bouncing, running, and laughing chorus of recess.

The young girl sat beside Phillip, who was now, after the confrontation, sitting on the wooden block edging that contained the base of a very solid, ancient oak, growing and stretching above them.

"Never mind that type, Phillip," she said. "They have a lot of polishing to go through in this life."

"Wait," Phillip quickly turned to her, his eyes meeting hers for the first time, noticing how clear and sparkling they were. "How do you know my name?"

"Like I said earlier," though when she said it this time it was much softer, "names aren't so important."

"Are you in my class?" He found himself unable to break away from her eyes.

"Yes…and no," she replied with a smile.

He tilted his head side-to-side like a puppy hearing whistling for the first time. "Yes and no," he repeated her coy words, smiling in return. "You are something, you know, standing up for me like that."

"I know! I am rather special." Now a full grin further lit up her eyes. "Can I tell you something, Phillip?"

Sensing the conversation going into waters away from the shore, like when his mom talked to him at times, Phillip looked hard at the little girl in the green dress. "Yes, I'm all ears."

"No matter what people say, Phillip—others, such as those boys—you must hold on to the light that is inside you."

He glanced away slightly. "You believe me, then…the candle inside of me…you believe, too?"

"I believe that, and a great deal more. I believe in you, Phillip, and I see that there are special gifts placed within you, building, drawing, writing....and much more inside, along with your candle."

Now she turned, running her hand over the mossy ground near the base of the ancient oak, and brought back, between their faces, pinched with the tip of her finger and thumb, an acorn.

"You see this?" focusing her dazzling eyes upon the acorn, then fixing them on the oak, "you see this great tree behind and above us? Well, it started from a small acorn, just like this one." She moved it around as if it were a diamond catching light. "As big, strong, and far reaching as this tree is, it all started from an acorn, a tiny seed of hope planted long ago."

She leaned back and patted the tree tenderly with her hand, her words velvet-like: "This tree has done good, really good... a lot of hope inside these branches."

The words reached deep within Phillip. He could sense them turning about, stirring, fluttering around inside him, and then landing down to a place deep inside of him, growing roots. He trusted her, and before he could filter his words they were already outside of him: "Did you see the light inside the teacher, when she was helping me?"

Smiling assurance, her eyes sparkling, she reached over and placed the acorn in the palm of his hand, then stood, brushing away the dirt from her dress. "I sure did, Phillip. I sure did." Turning, the girl walked away, and with a certain grace, she disappeared into the swirling symphony of noise and kids at play.

Phillip looked for her at school every day for a long time—down the halls, in other classes, and especially at recess—but he never saw the little girl with long brown hair and a green dress ever again.

Chapter 4

Meeting Dr. Lynn

Tabitha made certain Phillip looked his very best—polished dress shoes, belt, shirt tucked away evenly, tie straight—and even tamed his hair into order the best it would allow for. Standing and leaning back, she declared proudly, "Now you look sharp! Dr. Lynn will certainly have you at your very finest. You'll make for a great impression of what a young man should be like." She leaned further, then took a step back, pleased with her application of polish to what was normally a tangle of grass stains, muddy boots, and roughed-up kneecaps.

"Why do I have to see her, and especially like this?" He jerked his arms out and around as if the shirt, with its long row of buttons, was enchanted into shrinking tighter and tighter, in cahoots with the tie, to take his breath and leave him all polished up lying on the floor.

"Because you, my little love, have a candle inside of you, and she knows about such things. And from what Dr. Jenkins has informed me about Dr. Lynn, she very much wishes to meet you…so…," licking her fingers and pushing back into place a particularly stubborn shock of hair, "we are going to see her, and she, my sweet child, will meet us at our best."

"Oh, all right," Phillip agreed, resigning himself over to the plan of it all.

Tabitha continued messing with his hair, squinting her eyes back and forth and looking for areas still lacking in so-called "polish." "Dr. Jenkins will be here shortly to pick us up, so please don't dirty yourself…and Phillip…"

"Yes, mom," his brown eyes looked up at her.

"I love you. It will be a nice trip going into the City, and I am sure Dr. Lynn will be a very nice woman." Once again she bent to slick back the unruly patch of hair that was working hard to stand.

Tabitha walked hurriedly down the hall to finish her own polishing, and Phillip thought about her words of not getting dirty in his mind, imagining what would happen by just bending over to tie his shoes—a mess of shirt unfurling and buttons popping and zinging in all directions.

<hr>

The auditorium was full of people, most of whom Phillip saw to be looking their finest, all present to hear Dr. Lynn speak about the subject of inner light. When Dr. Lynn walked out on the stage, she looked altogether different from his imaginings. He had pictured her looking more like Dr. Jenkins, eyebrows and all, but she didn't look like him, instead being very tall, the straight, proud kind of tall. She wiped her blonde hair, trimmed short on the sides and longer in the front, away from her face and began to speak. At first she seemed anchored to the lectern that was centered, near the edge, mid-stage, but gradually loosened in long strides as she spoke. Phillip did not gather wholly what she was discussing, at times feeling like the true essence of what she was communicating to the audience was constructed of strange colors, colors he wasn't familiar with, colors he didn't have in his drawing pencil set, some words like the blues and greens he knew, others like the unexplored hues, the murky depths of purples mixed with red. Phillip sat watching, glancing around from time to time at those surrounding him to see if they too held these words within their palette, feeling that the bigger portion of the conversation was flowing, like a current, over his head. He sat up in his seat, pushing up from the thin cushion, an inch or two taller, trying to gather more because the bits and pieces he was capturing were colors he knew very well. He captured the sky blues and sun yellows of treating your fellow brothers and sisters with love, helping the poor and sick, offering aid to others in need, and many other ideas that he too felt, way down inside, and now listening to Dr. Lynn address the room with the paints that adorned the canvas of what he was made of, what he figured all good people, all people in fact, to be made of. The bits and pieces that he captured he liked, and from them he reckoned that all the buttons and stifling shirts in the world were worth it to be there.

After she completed her speech, there were those in the audience who applauded loudly, standing, and others, many others, who sneered their way out of rows into aisles, hushing under their breaths: "To think that there are candles in people, what's next?" Others sat quietly, still, not visible to one side or the other, wrestling on a tightrope with what had been said. Dr. Jenkins, Tabitha, and Phillip moved down the aisle, then another row, to a side door exiting the main auditorium. They were met by a large man who, by his stance, was watching over the door, the door to the room where Dr. Lynn was. After a brief word with the man, who entered the door for a quick moment then returned, Dr. Jenkins walked over to Tabitha and Phillip to explain that all was ready for them and that the man at the door had been put in place as a security precaution.

Dr. Lynn stood even taller in person, with a very bright, fair face, and a smile that encouraged everyone around to smile along, all the while with a seriousness that encouraged likewise. "Forgive the added security. I am finding that more and more there are those who are most opposed to the things of which I am called to speak of—but away from all that." Now she smiled again, stepping over, closer to the trio. "It's nice to meet you, Tabitha, and you," looking down at Phillip, "must be the young man with the candle."

She held out her hand and Phillip reached up, shaking it, holding it like it was expensive glassware. Dr. Lynn smiled once more. "Phillip, you don't have to be nervous. It's an honor to meet you and your mother…I may be tall but I am harmless."

She talked with Tabitha and Dr. Jenkins for a good long time, answering questions, searching through papers she had along with her, providing information of studies she had been conducting, occasionally looking over to Phillip, and back to the conversation. Phillip overheard stories of others like himself that Dr. Lynn had met here and there around the City, around the Town, and farther places he hadn't heard of. She mentioned candles, people who carried candles, people who didn't believe in candles, people who were dangerous who tried to extinguish candles, and she mentioned the Candle Maker, who made all the candles that were inside of the people she had met, sighing over the fact that regardless of her extensive research she had yet to meet the Candle Maker. The young boy listened intently at this, as if all the colors were laid out and he knew each one. He felt the warmth of his candle inside of him, and as he sat watching and listening to Dr. Lynn offer assurance to his mother and Dr. Jenkins, his eyes drifted downward, and there, shining in the middle of her chest, right where the heart resides, for just a moment, a candle was glowing within Dr. Lynn. Phillip lay down on the long chair, his head upon the cushion, smiling to himself, off into dreams full of colors—some he knew and some he would figure out later.

PART
TWO

Chapter 5

Snow

He continued growing, like the oak at recess, stretching beyond his roots, out of his home into friendships and adventures around the Town, discovering moments as they moved into months, into years. Phillip continued to dive into drawing, reading, writing, and building, bringing home book after book, studying, sketching, and designing many thoughts from his inner mind out into the world, his room an organized mess of papers, drawing pads, all sorts of plans tacked up to his wall, and structures of bridges and buildings that he built using cheap scraps of wood and glue. He was growing from his roots up and out into the wideness of discovery, into the murky purples and deep reds beyond his doorsteps.

He talked with his mother many times about attending the University, which lay at the center of the City, miles away from his home and from his mother, whose heart had grown with him and now was learning how to let go of the beautiful boy that had always been so near.

"Mom," Phillip held a piece of bread in one hand, wiping the crumbs away from his mouth with the other, "Mom…I have been thinking lately about what we talked about…or better what we didn't talk about the other night."

Tabitha, immediately recognizing his tone and intent, put down her book, knowing that it was finally time to let him know. "Yes, Phillip, I know, you want me to tell you."

Phillip, pleaded, "It's just that I want to know about him…I don't know that much, and…"

"I know, Phillip. I have been thinking about that quite a bit lately." She knew that her son had heard stories at school and around the Town. "Come, sit down. It's time we talked about your father." His mother reached over to try to gently push down a part of his hair that perpetually stood out and away. "Your father…my husband Eric…was indeed a wonderful man." Her arm retreated, acknowledging that Phillip's hair was made to stand on its own.

"I met him in school toward the middle of our last year there. He was studying art and I was in a reading class at the time. Our paths crossed here and there…and after a while he made sure they crossed quite often, every day in fact. We started spending our time together, walking during sunrises and sunsets, picnicking on the grass under the trees; he would show me all the sketches in his drawing pad...some of which were sketches of me. I knew that we were made to be together, two parts born separate but meant to connect and grow together. I took him as my husband at a small ceremony by the pond," her eyes now unfocused, lost back into the colors that made those days, greens of the grass and treetops along with the blue of the sky above, which was reflected from the surface of the pond that lived in her memory.

"Phillip...sometimes a person can feel things differently, more deeply than those around him. He was a heart, a walking, thinking, beating heart, which cared for all those around him, big and small. He felt joy profoundly and... he felt sadness in an equally powerful way. Your father felt things, all the things big and powerful in such a way....at times the weight of life was crushing to him."

"I heard," Phillip going into some of the stories he had been told, "that he and Dr. Jenkins were best friends...is that true?"

"Yes, quite true. Your father and Jeremiah grew up together, and many a mischievous romp did they have all around town. They were more like brothers I would say. Before Jeremiah went off to the University they were inseparable, laughing, thinking, going on and on into deep conversations about all sorts of topics, from bridge design to the complexities of the human heart. It was almost as if those two were one person, split to be in two different bodies."

Phillip looked sideways at his mother taking in the fact that his father once had and once was a best friend, something he hadn't thought of yet, not exactly knowing how to say what he wanted to say next, so he just opened up: "I heard stories that he had problems, Mom—trouble with drinking… and that he froze to death."

Tabitha's face nodded, hurt washing across her features. "Partly true…partly. You see…your father cared deeply for us, Phillip. He worked so hard to provide for us, so hard," wiping a stray tear that sneaked past her defenses to carry this conversation through without crying, she continued: "He wanted us to live a comfortable life, and it hurt him when he realized that he couldn't do what he wanted to do for us. He worked for a while at the lumber mill, hard long hours, and then they closed down for a time. So, he moved to the mines, which required him to wake up even earlier and return home later than before. This played on him tremendously…you see, Phillip, your father—my Eric—was made to create, to draw, to write. This life that he found himself in, apart from you and me, was harsh to him, and it played on him."

Looking into her son's eyes, she pressed on, determined to see the discussion through. "He began drinking, and drinking more, to hide from something or bury something, I can't exactly explain it. He was never abusive, never, Phillip,….he would just get quiet and many times go for long walks, as if he were trying to find something, a part of himself that had escaped outside somewhere. Jeremiah came back home and tried to help, we all tried to help, but there were caverns in your father, certain depths that we couldn't reach. One night he went for a walk, a very cold night, snow falling, and he was found the next day." This time she made no effort to wipe away a tear streaking down, letting it drop, letting it be.

Phillip didn't quite know how to take all of this, previously wanting to know for certain about his father, but now the knowledge was spinning inside of him, moving quickly, heating up. He felt sad, angry, relieved, all in a whirl, not knowing how to respond, not wanting to respond the way he did, but it just came out: "So my dad was a failure. He hid from his problems, and then died from them….all the things that I have been hearing at school are true." Not realizing he was standing and moving to the door, his face flushed with blood and heat, he walked outside and started walking away.

Chapter 6

Worn Shoes
and the
Lesson of Sight

Deflated, Phillip sat on a wooden bench looking out of spaced, unfocused eyes at the common area where people from the Town came to walk, picnic, and, in warmer weather, swim in the pond near the path. In his mind he conjured up images of his father, staggering along snow-swept streets, falling, freezing off into death, a failure. For a moment he hated his mother for not telling him before now, for holding back; he hated her for letting him know, hated the people of the Town for failing to hear and help, and hated his father most of all, whom he had never met, for his weakness. Blind in his thoughts, boiling into imagery of snow, death, and hatred, he failed to notice the scuffling

35

of feet as an older woman sat down beside him on the other end of the bench.

"Do bless, I am tired and my feet are mighty sore… mmm, mmmh, something sore," she spoke loudly enough for Phillip to hear.

Phillip, returning outward in his thinking, now noticed the old woman, old as anyone he had ever seen, under a myriad of layers against the late autumn wind and its chill. He crossed his arms as he edged away from her, closer to the outer edge of the bench.

"You do know," she said, obviously talking to him, "that I have walked many a step today, and of all the places in this land, I find myself right here, sitting right here, next to you." Her attention focused back on her feet. "Do bless these old feet of mine…mighty sore."

Phillip kept his position, stone-faced, staring forward, body rigid, hoping she would get the point and find somewhere to move along to with her complaining.

"Young man, I know you hear me," she persisted. "I swear… these young people these days…all rushed to get nowhere, all hurry up and wait, and then when they finally end up somewhere they can't see it."

She was now rubbing her knees. "Do bless these old legs of mine…mmm, mmm, mmmh, they are sore."

He broke the edge of his hard stare momentarily to glance, out of curiosity, at her feet, thinking that anyone hurting that bad must have something wrong with her. Her shoes looked beyond worn, older in style, along with the rest of her clothing, with scuffs severely worked into them, the soles worn bone-thin through what must have been countless, long, hard miles. Never in his life had Phillip seen such shoes; he could only imagine the path this lady had walked to end up beside him.

He softened, acknowledging her: "I'm sorry…I don't intend to be disrespectful to you, it's just that today I heard some bad news…and I just wanted to come here to sit and think for a while in quiet."

Still rubbing her knees, she corrected him: "Rude…"

He leaned closer. "Excuse me?"

"Rude, young man, you were being rude—not disrespectful. There's a difference between the two."

His face quite puzzled, mouth hanging open, Phillip stammered, "I…I…I'm sorry…I didn't mean to…"

"Hold it right there," putting her hand up, leathered by time but not frail, a thick finger stretched out, waving Phillip to stop speaking, "I know why you are here, Phillip. I was sent to find you."

Puzzled even more, he wondered who would have sent this woman shuffling along to find him. "I'm sorry, do I know you…"

"You are awfully sorry today, aren't you…and you know of me, a little bit about me, but not all of it, but enough to listen to what I have to say."

"Listen, I…I don't even know your name…"

Wagging a very old finger, unable to straighten it completely, she questioned, "Do you need to know the name of the bird in the tree behind us to pay attention and feel his song?"

Phillip, just now hearing the chirping melody, sharp, rhythmic, coming from the branches behind them, realized his heated thoughts had blocked out everything that was around him.

Still rubbing her knees, she continued, "You should know that names are something, something for sure, but far from being everything. Besides, you wouldn't be able to pronounce my name anyways." Again she mumbled to herself about how sorely her feet ached: "do bless these tired, worn feet of mine…mmm, mmmh, they hurt awful."

Phillip, looking at her shoes, was curious to learn more. "Ok, I am listening."

"Look out there, young man, in front of your face, and tell me what you see."

Breathing in, scanning around him, he focused his eyes on the scenery. "What is around me…ok…I see trees, benches, people walking."

"Do bless, mm, mmm, mmmh, child, you telling me that out there in front of your face, in all that world out yonder, you only see a few plants, chairs, and folk strolling along…mm, mmm, do bless."

The boy looked around more attentively as if he had missed something obvious, something important.

"Try again…try again, Phillip."

He breathed deeper, running his hands through his hair, looking harder, straining, thinking this time as he moved his eyes around him. "Tall trees, wide branches, close together, green canopy up top, stone-lined path, squirrels gathering food, a couple walking hand-in-hand, talking to each other," he turned to the old woman, quite pleased with his observation.

"Mmm, mm, mmmh…do bless this child." Her head tilted up to the sky. "Do bless him tremendously…so I hear you say, Phillip—let me know if I got this right—that you see, out there, in front of your own face, tall green plants, vermin getting food, and folk talking as they walk along."

His left hand flew straight up from rubbing his hair in complete frustration. "What am I supposed to see out there?!"

She wagged her crooked finger once more, back and forth to quiet his outburst. "Now that is disrespectful… mm, mm, mmm."

"Sorry…I'm sorry…I just don't see what you want me to see…." he sighed, stretching his arms dramatically out in front of him. "What's out there that I am not seeing?"

"Close your mouth, Phillip."

"What?" Phillip went back to rubbing his hair. "Come on…you can't be serious…."

"Close your mouth," her tone intensified.

Shaking his head, he followed along, closing his mouth, now silent.

"Now, close your eyes."

"What?" Phillip, another slip of impatience, but then he noticed her finger, back and forth, motioning for him to listen.

"Close your mouth and your eyes, young man."

Phillip, recognizing the tone again, followed, closing up his speaking and letting his eyelids slide down, ready to listen.

"Sometimes when we see something, or in your case Phillip, when we don't see something, we attach a whole fuss of our own thinking to what it is we're looking at. For instance, a slice of layered chocolate cake on a plate... this could be, through one mind of looking, a delicious after-dinner reward for making it through a long hard day on bad feet...or, through another window, it could be something else, it could be a memory of family, warmly gathered together, smiling all around, of a long-ago birthday celebration, in a house full of secure love...on a plate that proudly belonged to a young girl's mother. Both sets of eyes seeing the same thing, it's just that within the mind and heart, things are looked at differently, you see. Phillip, I want you to be honest with me, honest with what you see...I want you to say exactly what comes to your mind. Don't break it apart, just say what comes, ok?"

Phillip nodded, still holding his eyes closed. "Ok...I can do that."

"I know you can, now...I am going to say a word, just one single word, and you are going to let out everything, all the stuff inside of you, everything you have that goes along with that word." the old woman paused for a moment. "Are you ready, Phillip?"

Phillip nodded up and down.

"Ok...here we go...the word is..." she paused for a moment, "father."

He opened his eyes quickly as if she had pricked him with a needle. About to speak, he saw her finger wagging, so Phillip closed his mouth along with his eyes and let himself feel. The inside of Phillip begin to move, like the very ground under him was rumbling; he felt all sorts of things, good things, ugly things, all of which twisted and turned. His thinking escaped as words: "Snow…I see snow…the streets are so cold, wind blowing hard…my father, wrapped in failure, running from his problems, fleeing from my mother…and me…I see him falling, freezing, trying to get up but he's too drunk, falling again, nobody helping…not one person helping him, sleeping in warm beds…no one there…he's hurt…in pain…crying, tired, too tired to call out louder…so cold, freezing to death." Through closed eyes, tears now escaped from the corners of both eyes.

"Do bless….mmh, mm, mmm…that is something, something indeed, to have running all around in your head….so, is this…what you told me, what you saw…do you think that is the way it all happened?"

"I don't know…I just don't…" he noticed her finger again, this time more gentle, softly back and forth.

"Phillip, listen to me…this time I want you to try to see it differently, this time by candlelight." The woman raised both of her weathered hands up to the middle of her chest, right where the heart resides. "This time we are going to use our light to see what happened. Here's how I see it…your father worked hard for you and your mother, really hard, out of love, not burden. He was troubled by the fact that every cent had to be scraped for and then stretched so far. He wanted nicer things for you and your mother, and sometimes people twist it all up in a mess about what exactly nice things are...time...time, Phillip, being the most precious. Nevertheless, he loved you both dearly and it worked on him and haunted him sorely that you and your mother had to live in such a way...it worked on him through the long hard days and through the sleepless, worried nights."

Her tone was different now. "Did you know, Phillip, that he used to cradle you in his strong arms, just scoop you up, and take you on long walks when you were just a tiny little thing, just days old. Talking to you like you could talk back, about the geese that came and went by the pond near the path...the path right over there. He would talk to you about all sorts of things that went on in his mind...he too believed in candles...and he loved holding your little hands, so soft, he thought, never wanting them to grow hard like his."

Letting out a deep sigh, the old woman continued, "After the mine closed down, he felt like he had been taken apart, one cent being stretched to nothing, not being able to be stretched any more. Did you know, Phillip, that sometimes people can lose focus of what is right in front of them, good people...great, imaginative, loving people.....
He became haunted and started drinking. He wasn't a mean drunk by any means. He was just the type who drank to stop listening for a while, to soften a place deep, really deep, inside of him that was growing louder by the day. He got off, in a bad way one night, having too much to drink

and too many thoughts pounding at him, and needed to walk for a bit. He kissed your sleeping mother on the top of her dreaming head, right where her hair parts; then he ran his hard-worked hands ever so gently across your cheek and quietly closed the door behind him as he walked off into the snow. It was very late, Phillip, wind blowing, so nobody in Town heard him slip and fall, nobody…He hit his head on the stone walkway near the bakery and went to sleep dreaming with your mother…dreaming about you, Phillip…he fell asleep thinking about you."

His shoulders caved and he started to shake out, through broken breaths, many tears, warm, soft crying enveloping him, tears freeing themselves and freeing Phillip along with them. His eyes the cage, now opened, releasing strange birds into the high branches that surrounded them, strange tears that had fluttered within him for a long time.

Trying to speak with solid words his voice was still shaky: "How do you know…how do you know these things?"

The old woman paused for a quiet moment. "It's just the way I see them, Phillip, just the way I see them." Half standing, she rubbed her knees and then fully stood. From the far side of her, away from Phillip, she reached for and moved out in front of her a thin, long stick and began tapping at the ground in front of her feet, slowly shuffling away from the bench, mumbling to herself, "Do bless these tired, hurting feet…mm, mmm…do bless."

Phillip, his relaxed breathing working through him, his body no longer holding tension, wiped his eyes and watched her, slowly walking, tapping the stick softly in front of her, small measured step after step, each one rubbing across the ground. With a certain grace, she shuffled on down the path, never to be seen again.

Chapter 7

Out the Door

Phillip made his way back home before sunset that evening. He hugged his mother dearly, cried upon her shoulders, and apologized for storming out. They talked late into the night about good things, about old memories, detailed stories about her time with Phillip's father, pleasant stories filling up the small kitchen illuminated by candlelight.

Time continued burning away as is its nature, while Phillip continued his studies and his relationships—with friends, with himself, and with all the world around him— growing out like far-reaching branches. He applied for and was accepted to attend the University, which was miles and miles away from his home and located in the City.

Tabitha, searching daily within her heart for the strength, understood that the time was near for Phillip to step out beyond their home, out beyond the Town, to carve his own path. Understanding is different than accepting, and she found it harder each day to watch him move closer to the moment of walking out the door off into the City to further his studies. She knew he would be fine, more than fine, but it was a thought that held a certain type of sad sweetness about it, her precious baby boy on the doorstep of manhood, on the cusp of independence, on the ledge of leaving to find his own peace in the vast world full of sound and colors.

The day came, more swiftly than she would have liked, but nevertheless, he stood before her, his bags packed and lined up near the front door.

"You know, the door will always be open for you," she said, reaching up to try once more to fold into place the unruly cord of hair sticking up.

"Yes, mom, I do know that. And for you, please know that you have done a marvelous job performing as a mother, a listener, and a friend." He leaned down to kiss her cheek and hug her. "Of all the mothers in the world, I have been provided with the finest."

She smiled in reply, eyes watering. "You are an amazing boy, Phillip." Bringing the palm of her hand to rest on his chest, she advised, "Guard what's inside— take care of your light and it will always take care of you." Wiping her eyes, she changed her voice to offer gladder tidings: "Now, off you go! You are going to be late for your travels…and know that you better write as soon as you can."

Grabbing his packed bags, stepping out the door, looking back to his mother, his home—his whole life up until this point—he bid his farewell: "I love you mom…I will visit soon and write even sooner." Phillip stepped from one life into another, all the while thinking about the candle's worth of flame glowing in his chest.

Chapter 8

University

Learning had always been a passion for Phillip, and now he was immersed in a life where each day was balanced on the scales of discussion, discourse, and debate of all manner of topics. He was enrolled in design courses that analyzed building methods, writing classes that challenged him to go into who he was—sifting the soil of his experience, to come back to the surface with treasure to be laid out in word on paper—and art classes, where he was allowed the freedom to find form and bend color onto canvas. Phillip thoroughly enjoyed his days, making friends and connecting to people from faraway places who held within them entirely different ideas and thoughts, all the while having the similar shades that all people carry, such as a desire to grow, a need to be appreciated and have their voices find sanctuary inside of others, and with each breath, the longing to be loved.

He was very fond of his early morning walks around the campus, appreciating the green of the sweeping lawns, and the tower, with its bell that chimed hourly, sending its brass echoes into the trees that lined the walkways full of songbirds—all of this Phillip loved to take in along with the sunrise. He joined a poetry club that met twice weekly after classes to talk about the words and works of others they studied, and it also provided the opportunity to share individual writings— a safe place to open up, a place to let others know the depths of canyons within, and to listen and connect to the far reaches within others. Phillip continued to write home often, and through his correspondence with his mother kept her up to date on all the sunshine pouring into his life, all of which he wanted her to see and feel as well. He was well within himself and he felt his candle, warm, burning, coursing through him.

He began to speak through his poetry sessions about the candle within and found that others were intrigued by the thought. Phillip opened up more and more about what he thought and felt, sharing his experience with others in the group. It was here in this moment that he planted acorns, forming a group within a group, for those who really opened up to the notion of candlelight residing in the heart of a person. They called the group "The Candles," simple yet profound. He did not know it yet but he was planting something, something that would one day grow to provide shade for him.

Many ideas were tossed around during the different meetings he attended, with the poetry group, with The Candles, within classes, over picnics on the lawns, and it was during one of these discussions, lunch spread out on a blanket under a particularly dense section of trees, that Phillip first heard of Bright Light.

Phillip, along with a few friends, were enjoying their meal, sharing stories and laughter, when two students came up to speak to them.

"Hello", said the first student, standing, one hand in his pocket, one hand holding a stack of papers, flyers to be passed around for an event they were promoting. "Do you mind if we join you?"

"Not at all," responded one of Phillip's friends. "Please have a seat. We were just having a meal and deciding on how to solve all the problems from the beginning of time to its conclusion." At this, sincere chuckling broke out from those sitting, for they were a group that talked frequently of problems and possible solutions, and it wasn't lost upon them the gravity of finding answers to the issues they intellectually grappled with.

The first of the two, looking around, smiled again. "Well, we are more at home than we thought!" Both sat down, almost in unison. "You see, we are walking around today, inviting others to come hear the message of Bright Light." On this cue, the other one began passing out flyers around the circle of friends.

"Bright Light," mused one of Phillip's friends, one whom he met and grown close to during a creative writing class, "the name sounds familiar."

The second person of the two spoke up: "Perhaps you have heard his name from one of his speeches. He is currently moving across the land, informing people about the true path to freedom...the true path to freeing the inner light. You see, he is the leader of a movement of free thinking."

At this comment Phillip looked at the flyer closely, noticing a strange symbol printed at the bottom of the sheet, then back to the two to say, "What do you mean by freeing the inner light?"

Both now smiled at Phillip, and the first one spoke again: "It sounds as if you are intrigued. Well...as the flyer states, he will be here in a few weeks' time and it could benefit you." Both looking around at the group, and the second one added, "It would greatly benefit all of you to attend." Just as abruptly as they had joined the seated group, the two strangers stood and parted, leaving behind a small pile of flyers, each marked with a symbol that caused Phillip to feel slightly uneasy. Phillip read over the one in his hands carefully, noting the bottom line on the paper: *For those who hold light, I alone will help you understand. I alone can free you.* He was definitely interested and tried to shrug off his initial unrest. He folded the paper and placed it in the front of a book he was reading, a book about the crafting of stained glass.

Chapter 9

Bright Light

T he auditorium was full, each seat, row after row after packed row, full beyond capacity. Phillip couldn't find a place to sit, so he began making his way to the back, stepping around others sitting in the aisles. Looking around, amidst a cacophony of voices one on top of the other, he recognized many faces: a few from his classes, a couple here and there from the poetry group, others that he did not know but remembered seeing around campus, and even a face he recognized from home. Along with him, standing in the back, were a few of The Candles. All the voices, jumbled as one, hushed to quiet as the lighting dimmed in the auditorium, dimmed further, then faded out completely, into darkness.

Faint light opened up near the front of the stage, growing then recognizably brighter, as a group of around twenty people, some coming from the left side of the stage, some from the right, walked up slowly, each dressed in white, each holding, at arm's length, a burning candle. Each placed his or her candle near the front of the stage, equally spaced along its ledge, and still in patterned strides, they walked off the stage opposite the side they had entered. From the sectioned-off area directly in front of the stage, low pulsing drumming began, followed by thin, whispery string music. Phillip could see that the musicians were dressed identically to those who had placed the candles out around the front of the stage. Then, as suddenly as it had begun, the music stopped, and out of the unlit darkness that blanketed the back of the stage, unnoticed before, walked a slightly taller-than-average man with richly blonde hair, curled and resting upon his shoulders, wearing white, though he had a bright yellow, almost golden, sash from his left shoulder to and around his waist. He was Bright Light.

After welcoming the audience he began to speak, his arms rising and falling fluidly, sometimes swaying his hands back and forth with long fingers flexing and bending to accent his phrases. The way in which he moved his arms reminded Phillip of how the conductors held command over their orchestras during the Music Department's concerts at the University. His wand-like motions gestured, encircled and intertwined with his words as if he were pushing them out and around the audience, who were all listening intently, watching, taking it all in. Bright Light moved about the stage in long certain strides, sometimes elaborately bending and stretching, his voice expanding and contracting, a pulse of words. There was a certain quality, a faint, mist-like attribute that danced along with his speaking, filling up the great room. The cadence of Bright Light's tone, the movement of his gestures, accompanied here and there by the low thin music, all of it caressing Phillip's thinking, lulling him.

He felt a sharp nudge in his ribs by the student beside him, whom he didn't recognize at all, not sure when she came to stand next to him. "Listen, Phillip," she whispered, "listen to what he's really saying."

Phillip glanced down at the stage, then back to the young lady, now noticing her red hair. "Excuse me…do I know you?" he whispered in response, leaning in close to speak, amazed at just how remarkably green her eyes were.

She held up a finger to her lips. "Just listen, Phillip, really listen to what he is saying. Sometimes you need to look beyond words to sense what someone is really saying." For emphasis, she moved her hand from her mouth to the center of her chest, right where the heart resides. She then turned, moving with a certain grace, shouldering her way through the dense crowd of listeners near the back wall, never to be seen again.

He began listening, pushing through the low pulsing music, pushing through the dramatic show of movement and exaggerated motions, through the front of it all into the words themselves, into what was really being said. He closed his eyes, listened, and began to feel what was really being said. It was almost as if Bright Light was speaking directly to Phillip while simultaneously speaking to every single person gathered in the auditorium. Phillip pushed through this, noticing that the words were moving around a portion of himself, deep inside, to another part of him, a long buried part. This curving trick of words sought to stir within Phillip something from an inner cavern, something that was supposed to remain buried under rock, entombed. Bright Light released sentence after sentence to the audience, strange sentences, all attempting to land, to stir, to take root in places they had no permission to dwell. Phillip kept his eyes closed and listened to what was really being said.

"The true path toward fulfillment in this life...towards truth...already resides inside of you...inside each of you. You know what you want, all of your desires...all of the inner hungers that gnaw at you...you feel them, you listen as they speak...as I speak....I tell you honestly, there is cleansing in chasing these desires. I tell you honestly, there is great discovery in giving yourself over to these emotions....I tell you honestly, we are all born masterless, born to be masters over our own thinking, over our own fulfillment, over our own desires...we become the masters of our own destinies by giving ourselves, our inner light, over to these feelings, a song...giving yourself over to a beautiful song, becoming a part of its chorus. You do not bow down to what is inside of you; it bows down to you, and you feed your emotions through thought, and more importantly, through actions. We are our own rulers, each a king or a queen, charting our own course through life, each holding majesty over the light, over our hearts. Higher powers to which we are indentured to serve....I tell you honestly, this is a myth, a fairy tale constructed by those before you who held on to their ignorance and lack of understanding about the true constructs of this land. You....I say again, you are the higher power, you, each of you, are all capable to live above such foolish ideology. You were born to look down upon your own lives, holding within your own hands the abilities to build, break, give, and take...take all that you want, break all that you want...there is a freedom I offer to you, honestly, freedom of thought, freedom of speech, freedom of action, freedom of pleasure, freedom from servitude to laws that you weren't meant to abide by...pleasure doesn't lead to pain...it leads to possibilities. I honestly tell you we do not serve a greater light other than the very light that is within us, which is made to consume... which longs to search out and find through experience the desires of what is inside. Are we made to be a flicker? Of course not. Honestly, I tell you, we are made in the image of ourselves to find in this land, the only land we will ever know, the freedom to consume and be consumed by others...each day exhausted within our deepest, innermost longings. I tell you honestly, there is no power above you, no power above me, and that we are masterless. That is why I am here, to give you such freedom, to show you a path through the lies that you may have been told, the chains you may have holding you down. I tell you honestly, I am here to show you this path to freedom, to the only real happiness you will ever know. I offer this to you, to each of you, to follow me. There are great oceans of pleasure in this land....I require nothing, nothing at all, honestly, only the decision to follow me, to dive headfirst from the cliff of where you now live and breathe to land within me, unharmed, upon the soft blankets of the peace I can offer… riches I offer…luxury I offer…fame I offer…a life worth living I offer…pleasure I offer…no more struggle with the notion of restraint. If you seek power, then seek power through my path….if you seek pleasure, then seek pleasure through me…if you seek life, then seek life through me. I honestly tell you, there is no master but you and you are enough to bring this life to its knees before you to take what you wish. This I offer. I am the Bright Light of this land, your liberator, and I have come to set you free."

Bright Light turned and walked back into the dark recesses of the stage, folding away into the shadows, as low, thin music once again worked up from in front of the stage. Sporadically, then in unison, many people stood, people Phillip knew, some from classes, some from his poetry group, some near him, a few of The Candles, and began to applaud wildly. Others sat, remaining still, inwardly spinning around in their mind the words that were said, twirling them around like a tuft of loose string in the cuff of a sweater. Phillip noticed that some shook their heads side-to-side, disbelieving what was spoken.

Phillip began to make his way out of the auditorium and realized just how heavy the words were sitting in his throat and stomach. Rotten and twisting, Bright Light's speech worked within him, bringing him to nausea. Phillip, now worked to the point of throwing up, moved through the throng of people exiting as he frantically searched for a bathroom. Down the hall, then turn, another turn, then another down a longer hall, until finally finding what he sought. He burst into a stall, feeling cold and clammy, as his stomach wretched, vomiting out against the poison of words, the poison of spoiled promises, the poison of people he knew taking it into their veins…deeper yet into places, sacred places, way down inside, through seals that were never meant to be broken. Empty of the poison and feeling much better, Phillip placed both hands into a water basin and splashed his face several times. Rubbing damp hands on the back of his neck, he stared into the mirror at his reflection, wondering how people could allow such words to land within them. His stomach was still tilted and uneasy as he timed his breaths, in…out, slowly…in…out, slowly…in…out, slowly…and there, in the middle of his chest, right where the heart resides, he could see his candle, still lit, glowing, pulsing with his breathing, up and down. Just as it appeared it faded from view, now just a buttoned-up shirt and gray vest for special occasions.

Phillip realized, stepping back into the unfamiliar hall, that he was indeed lost amid the bends and corners of marble flooring and wall pictures of prestigious figures that helped in their own special way to establish the University. He decided that all halls would eventually lead to an exit and started off to find his bed and sleep off what he felt. Phillip noticed after several turns a gathering of people down a corridor, all huddled around and going into an open side door above which hung a strange, darkly painted decoration, a wreath of sorts that was all thorns with no flowers and hurtful looking. Admittedly, he was curious, so he walked by the open door. He saw a single file line down the side of the room's far wall, and at the very front he saw Bright Light standing on a slight platform with strange symbols etched around the base. Phillip recognized a few of the faces in line, watching them, one by one, stepping up to meet Bright Light and then whispering something up toward him. Bright Light would then bend down to whisper something in reply, and then, to Phillip's astonishment, each person would then put a hand to his or her chest and then pull that hand away, the palm now holding a candle's worth of flame out toward Bright Light, who would reach down to receive the light to the palm of his hands and then move it toward his chest where it was seemingly absorbed. Phillip watched this process more than once, completely bewildered as one by one, person after person, soul after soul, a flame was given over to Bright Light. Phillip noticed that as these individuals walked out of the room, he was unnoticed to them, and they all seemed like husks of what and who they were just moments before, carrying emptiness behind their now hollow eyes. The emotions stirred within him and before he could catch his feet or his words, he pleaded, "Stop...Stop...please STOP!" A young man, similar in age to Phillip, now holding a flickering spark in his hands and reaching out to give it over to Bright Light, looked over to Phillip, as did the entire room, along with a subtly grinning Bright Light. Phillip found himself rushing up and then pushing himself between the two, cupping the young man's hands, easing them back and pressing the light against the youth's chest. He watched in astonishment as the light worked its way back to whence it was taken, its sacred home.

Bright Light's grin widened as he spoke out across the room: "That will be all for tonight. Please find your way home and have no worries because our paths will cross again soon enough."

The young man's eyes met Phillip's, then broke aside to look into the face of Bright Light before settling back on Phillip. A trembling "thank you" was all he could muster as he pulled away and slipped out the door with the dispersing group.

The room with the strange decoration on the door was empty now with the exception of Phillip and Bright Light, who spoke first. "Well, dear Phillip, I suppose that the education of manners is not in abundance where you were raised. You rudely interrupted my evening."

"How do you know my name?" Phillip stammered in response, now noticing how striking Bright Light's features were and how his eyes were a smoky blue that seemed to on and off again pulse to darker shades of gray and back again. Phillip forced out of shaking lips, "And why are you taking light from people?"

"First of all, dear Phillip", Bright Light said as he stepped from the platform, "names are child's play. And as for the second question you posed, let's come to an understanding right now. I don't take anything from anyone. It is freely given, just as you saw." Bright Light's eyes danced in their strange way of blue to gray and back again as he continued walking slow-paced circles around Phillip. "The way I see things, Phillip, is like this: if something is given, freely given, over to me, I can do with it as I so please. And, Phillip, it pleases me very much to blot out each bit of flame that is handed over."

Phillip suddenly noticed how cold the room was. He looked at Bright Light, trying to respond to this shocking admission, and that's when he saw it. Instead of Bright Light having a candle right there in the middle of his chest, where the heart normally resides, Phillip noticed darkness, beyond darkness, churning, spinning, a void that held no light and seemed wickedly hungry to twist and extinguish light.

The grin on Bright Light's face stretched open. "If it is freely given to me, Phillip, as you witnessed, it is mine to scratch, mine to claw, and mine to break."

Phillip, strongly nauseous again, felt like falling into a heaving and shivering pile on the floor, yet he stood, divinely braced by unseen hands. He responded forcefully, "You were speaking against the Candle Maker, and you dare to steal light from others." Looking up into Bright Light's face, he added, "No good end will find you."

The grin turned sharply to a sneer, and Phillip noticed that mentioning the Candle Maker stirred something, as Bright Light's eyes rolled from gray to a smoky-orange color. An angry reply followed, "I steal nothing. I don't have to steal. Phillip, you speak of your so-called Candle Maker as if you know something of candles, of light, of giving and stealing. You, Phillip, know nothing, serve nothing, and are nothing just like your father who was nothing before you and died a cold-shamed nothing death in the nothing streets of your nothing town. You are dust, made of dust, serving a master of dust…you have no proof to offer, no evidence, not even a shred to put forth in the sake of this so-called Candle Maker that you speak and dream of."

Terribly weak now, Phillip braced himself on a nearby support pillar. He felt his legs giving way beneath him, but he felt moved again to stand and once more to speak. He noticed a warm feeling within his chest as if his candle were brightening in anticipation of what he was about to say: "You who are empty of light, forever parted from peace, know that you hold no power over me, for the light that I have been given is a reflection of the master who made it, the Candle Maker, both of which are unbreakable. Once again, I say to you and your soured depths, no good end will find you."

The wicked sneer fell from Bright Light's face, his eyes shifting in smoky colors, and then the grin returned. "Words and dust, Phillip, that is all that you are and all you will ever be. Now, if you will excuse me, I have business elsewhere that requires my full attention. Be mindful, Phillip, on which side you play—be very mindful." Bright Light gathered a few things from off a nearby table into a satchel and walked out of the room and down the hall.

Phillip's unsteady knees caved and he collapsed upon the floor, shivering and sickened by the exchange, taking a long while to regain his bearing enough to weakly stand and find his own way out of the building.

Chapter 10

Hope's
Morning Song

The birds were singing and the mist of the morning slowly lifted away to the sunrise, which was spilling gentle light through the canopy of trees. Phillip enjoyed his morning walks around the University, especially the span he was now on, which was shrouded by towering oaks. It was here that he first heard Hope's morning song, a gentle bittersweet melody floating through the falling bars of sunlight and the green foliage stretching out in all directions around him. Phillip paused and tilted his head sideways as puppies do when hearing curious sounds, trying to place the song, and there, off the path, sitting against the base of an oak, was a beautiful young woman sketching on a tablet of paper singing to herself.

Phillip watched for a moment as she continued singing out to the trees that stood protectively surrounding her, and to the birds that had no choice but to be swept away by such a sweet melody, joining her voice in chorus.

Before he could register what to do, he found himself only steps away from her. She looked up and it was here that Phillip discovered the purity of her eyes, eyes that looked into him and knew something.

"Um…hello…beautiful song that you're singing," Phillip fumbled.

"Thank you. It is a morning song, one that my mother taught me when I was a child. My name is Hope, "she said, with a smile that could light up a room.

Phillip, staring back at this wonderful creation with long brown hair and eyes that told the stories he longed to hear, realized that a long moment had passed in silence. "Sorry…I am Phillip…I mean my name…my name is Phillip…Phillip is what I am called," he sputtered, feeling quite clammy. "I walk quite often and love the morning air." He paused to look up through the treetops. "Something about greeting each day as it is born helps me feel like I haven't missed anything, like I am part of it all." Looking back at her, he felt fortunate that something somewhat eloquent finally worked its way out.

"I know how you feel," Hope replied. "I like witnessing the birth of a new day as well." She looked up toward the trees, joining Phillip's gaze, "You're right Phillip—there is something beautiful about meeting the day at the door of morning."

Phillip realized that yet again he was stuck in silence, admitting to himself that he was awestruck by the poetic nature and raw beauty of Hope. A song singing a song, he thought to himself.

Standing and brushing specks of grass from her turquoise dress, Hope commented, "I bet you are a great writer, Phillip. Anyone who walks around looking for a day to begin has to have words twirling around inside."

"Well...I...um..." The words fell apart on his tongue before figuring their way back. "I do write a bit. I am part of a group of people that meet to talk about things...things of the heart...and we often share words we have captured."

"That you have captured? That is an interesting way to view writing," Hope responded from behind a coy, yet very warm grin.

Phillip got lost again in her eyes. "Yes...I mean sure... ideas and feelings all the time working around in the depths of a person, and at times, quiet and still times, a person can think them through into words and onto paper...I have found it's all about being quiet and still long enough to think them through..."

"I know what you are talking about, Phillip." Hope spoke with both her voice and her eyes. "There is something special about silence and stillness....I like to think of ideas as butterflies fluttering around in a garden of memory, full of many different flowers planted through time and through many different experiences. Like you say, if a person is still and quiet long enough, and mindful, these butterflies land nearby, sometimes in the shape of song, sometimes in lines of words, and in my case, through drawings."

Hope now opened up her drawing pad to a page that held within its edges a most glorious drawing of a butterfly perched upon a hand holding a pencil, with a garden of flowers in the background. Phillip marveled at the detail within Hope's drawing, almost imagining the wings flexing to lift the butterfly from its perch to land on the nearby petals. Phillip looked at the drawing and then at Hope, marveling at her as well, thinking about such a wonderful creation, singing and drawing to the breath of morning under trees that seem like they were born to offer her shade.

Phillip looked back at the drawing and mumbled to himself but loud enough for Hope to hear, "A garden of memory..."

"That's not such a bad title," Hope spoke and smiled. "A Garden of Memory...I think that will work as the title for this sketch."

She closed the book and picked up a denim backpack leaning against the tree. "I am off to my first class of the day."

"Art?" Phillip asked.

Through a smile, perhaps the loveliest smile he had ever gazed upon, she answered, "Oh no, not my first class. First I have literature. We are reading fairy tales, and today it's my turn to speak about a lovely story of two people falling in love the very first time they meet."

Phillip actually nodded forward and slipped a bit. "Really? I mean...I mean that is quite some story."

"Really, Phillip." Still smiling, she took a few bouncing steps down the path, back toward the University.

"Will I see you again? I mean, can I see you again?" Phillip grimacing as the words, the whole idea, bobbled around and fell right out of his mouth.

Again, a sea of eyes, smile, and turquoise dress answered him: "I sure hope so."

Phillip leaned an arm out to the oak beside him to catch his balance. He noticed, as she turned back with a parting smile, that right in the middle of her chest, where the heart resides, a candle burned brightly. A smile washed over his face, complete and giddy, as a small tide rippled through him from the ocean he had just experienced.

Chapter 11

The Wind of Angel Wings

P hillip and Hope spent their days within the warmth of each other's company. Hand-in-hand, strolling, talking together, and giggling under oak trees upon a blanket, they spilled out words that the depths of their hearts held and wanted to hold and wished to release. Every day was sunlight for them, and each night full of stars they grew closer, like two pieces of cord spinning around and around each other being mended together as one.

They found themselves quite often aimlessly wandering the streets past the storefronts of the City, just passing time with each other and walking amongst the heavy lines of people going places or coming from where they had been. It was something Phillip and Hope enjoyed, all the hustle and bustle opened up something for them that they then poured into drawings, poetry, and discussions with their friends over coffee. Phillip sent letter after letter home to his mother about his new life at the University, about his work and all he was learning, and about Hope. He had made plans to visit her very soon with Hope, and this idea very much delighted Tabitha, who was proud of him and was excited to see for herself all the tremendous qualities that Phillip wrote about with such endearment.

On this particular day, the pair decided to walk into a shop that was known for its unique and creative pottery and sculpture designs. Local artists would create their work and display and sell it at this location. The window was full of vases, small and large bowls, and sculptures of various designs, all with the mark of a master's touch, each holding an essence of quality and command of an idea expressed.

"What do you think this is?" Hope asked Phillip, playfully squinting up her face into a smile.

"Definitely a unicorn," Phillip innocently smirked in reply, as the abstract and multi-colored glazed sculpture resembled nothing remotely close to a unicorn.

"Really? I was thinking it was more along the lines of an interpretive work, perhaps the artist's representation of emotion, or should I say, judging by the spectrum of colors used, the depths and range of emotion that a human being is capable of...and being the piece was made to be rather formless, I do believe the artist," holding the piece upside down now to reveal the artist's name, "in this case, I believe Manpreet Namaste, if I am saying the name correctly, is speaking to the very nature of emotion itself and its ambiguity and rather elusive nature to exact from the formless into concrete understandings." She smiled at Phillip, whose face in return was tilted into a perfect balance of affection and wonder.

He smiled a bit deeper at her and said, "Well, that is one interpretation but to me...I am still feeling like it's a unicorn."

"Perhaps, Phillip, although I think we can be at odds on this one," Hope bantered back with eyes flashing smiles and admiration.

At this the shop door chimed open as a friend from the University ran up to the couple, breathless and panting, completely opposite of the still tranquil setting of fine and delicate works surrounding them.

"Phillip...sorry to barge in like this...my friend... word came to the University today to your hall..." and the next words felt like large, jagged stones pushed into Phillip's inner waters, dropping, cutting to the depths of his spirit, sinking down to a murky bottom he did not know laid deep down within him. "Your mother...your mother, Phillip...your mother has passed."

Hope squeezed his hand, holding on to keep Phillip from sinking, then embraced him, and there they both stood leaning onto and into each other, weathering a wind that had blown so sudden, bitter, and hard.

"I am sorry, Phillip...I was told to come get you quick...I am sorry...so sorry...the hall master is waiting to speak with you and set up travel back home." And just like that the bell chimed on the door and such a sudden, breathless wind passed from them, leaving the pair in its wake, Phillip's mind conjuring up stories he had heard of sudden wind storms that funneled right out of the sky, so sudden, so destructive, and so quickly gone back into the sky…silence one moment, then so swiftly disaster, and then quiet again, the survivors left to pick up the pieces broken all around.

The couple didn't move for long moment, just holding onto each other in the middle of the store.

The owner, having heard everything, slowly approached the pair, not knowing exactly how to begin to explain what he needed to. Not really knowing what to say or how to start, he decided to just clear his throat.

"Uhmm…umm…excuse me…I overheard what just happened and I wanted to let you know that I am sorry about your loss, young man. I know that in times like these, words…words fall rather short." He glanced to the back of the store and back to the pair. "We…we had a piece come in just last night, quite an amazing piece, and…I really don't know how to explain…but as strange as this sounds, the artist wished to remain anonymous…but there was a note, rather instructions…instructions for me to give the piece away. I was told in the letter that I would know when and to whom to give it, and I am certain it was sent to find you, to find you here today." The owner backed away slowly, then quickened his pace back to the room behind the counter, and then slowly walked back out holding an exquisite figure. It was masterfully shaped, more than a foot tall, into the form of an angel reaching up with both hands skyward with wings beautifully outstretched. The finish was an opaque pearl color that had been applied in such a way so that the figure shined, polished so that it faintly radiated light. It was obviously the work of a lifelong artist, whose skill and eye were beyond refined and capable, a masterpiece created by a master, and it captured everything beautiful, loving, and graceful that angels are, like a song being sung heavenward.

The owner gently handed it over. "Although the artist did not reveal a name in the letter, the work itself does have a name." Feeling flushed with the strange joy that accompanies profound mysteries and revelations, the owner began to cry as he told Phillip, "the letter stated that it...it is titled, 'The Mother'…truly it is a gift for you, young man." And all three wept around the angel, through the devastation of great loss, of things left unsaid, visits left undone, and the depth of mysteries—all three wept around the angel who reached up from them toward heaven.

Chapter 12

New Life

After the funeral, time passed rather quickly for Phillip and Hope. There is a sadness that invites itself in with the loss of a loved one, but there is also new life opening and unfolding all around. It took time for Phillip to come to peace with the passing of his mother, but within his spirit lived fond memories of care, guidance, and love that transcended the distance of heartbeats. The angel sculpture was kept on the mantel, and it frequently reminded him that there were deeper laws at work than loss and that these deeper laws were part of his path, behind him, ahead of him, and within him.

It was on a sunny midsummer day that Phillip led Hope down by the shade of the trees in which they first met. They spoke upon a blanket, head lying next to head, both looking up and talking about tree canopies and the way light spilled down like honey-tinted water over leaves hanging their green heads in prayer as the sun filled them with life, new life. It was here that Phillip became silent for a long pause.

"Are you ok?" Hope asked.

Phillip rolled his head over, looking eye to eye into Hope. "Oh...of course. I was just thinking about something."

"About light and trees...that is enough to spend lifetimes on," Hope responded, softly smiling.

Philip looked at her smile, her soft lips, her teeth, the corners of her mouth flickering. "No...not really about trees and not necessarily light...I was thinking more about lifetimes."

"Lifetimes?" Hope said, questioning, lifting to rest upon one elbow.

"Yes...lifetimes." At this Phillip turned, reached into his worn leather pack, and brought out a sketchbook.

Hope anxiously peered at the book, now sitting to full attention. "Phillip, what is this?"

Phillip began to smile, "Lifetimes...you know...well, let me show you," and he opened the book to reveal a drawing of Hope's hand. "You know that I have held your hand so much that I could draw it from memory. See, I even got the freckles right."

Hope looked at the sketch and then at her own hand, back to the drawing and then back to her hand, mouth slightly open, more than smiling.

"Also", he turned the page to another drawing, "this is you as you were sleeping that one night…remember, when you fell asleep on the long chair? I think that night we were talking with friends about new methods in creating stained glass and ways to put all the pieces together so the whole window would last longer…I think that conversation put you to sleep."

"Yes, I remember…stained glass…I was so tired that night, and you guys were on that topic for a good long while."

"I know. You fell asleep right there…but it was late….I remember that before I woke you to walk you home, I just watched you for a long time as you slept. I wanted to remember it….your long hair was," Phillip was talking with his hands at this, trying to find the right words to capture what he really wanted to express, "your hair was drifting down on and across the cushion like a river, a deep auburn river….your hand was cupped underneath your head and your hair covered everything but your fingertips. I watched you because I didn't want to forget."

Hope looked at the drawing and the detail was immaculate, the folds in Phillip's jacket that he placed over her as a blanket, the texture of the cushion, even down to the fingertips and her hair. Her mouth now pursed and her eyes began to water, warm water, as she could feel light rising within her.

"And this next page is what I imagined you were dreaming of that night." He turned the page to a beautiful watercolor painting of dreamlike quality, a setting of light pouring down from stained-glass windows onto a field of grass with trees stretching all around. Beneath one tree was Hope, eyes lifted up, allowing the soft blue light from the windows to dance upon her face as if she were singing to the stars and moon overhead.

"Phillip…I don't know…what can I say…." Surprised and now holding both of his hands, she felt warm water tears streaking down the corners of both eyes.

Phillip looked into her eyes, still dazzling despite the tears, and down to her hands in his hands. "About lifetimes…." he turned the page a final time to reveal another drawing of her hand, this time wearing an intricately designed yet elegant silver ring.

He let the moment sink in, as she pulled both hands to her mouth and began sobbing, quaking with happiness and joy, shaking her head up and down. "Yes…Yes, Phillip…I will marry you!"

Tears now escaped Phillip as he reached into his pack to bring forth the same silver ring that was in the sketch. He gently and lovingly placed the ring onto her finger. They held each other on the outstretched blanket, both allowing tears to run their course, underneath oak limbs stretching and reaching out, under the choir of birds singing songs of wonder down upon them. There in that moment, they held each other with their arms, with their hearts, and with their souls, two people finding each other and becoming as one.

Chapter 13

Room for Three

They were married soon after his proposal, and together they moved into a small cottage near enough to the City and yet far enough away. It was full of shelves that were full of books. There were plenty of trees, trees of all sorts, in the yard, and there was even a small window in the kitchen area that Phillip had surprised Hope with, a mixture of green and blue shards making a beautiful stained-glass window that allowed light to fall directly upon the table during early morning coffee. Their days were full of laughter, long discussions during strolls around the Village and through the forests surrounding the street on which they lived, and love for each other and all things beautiful. They were both in their final year of learning at the University, Phillip pouring himself into building design of all sorts, from bridges to great halls, and Hope completing her studies in the art of written language, from poetry to dissertations by classic authors and their long ago, yet time-spanning thoughts. Together they lived, studying late into evenings, laughing over dinners with friends, their house an open ground for ideas and possibilities.

It was over a cup of coffee one morning, early enough so that the table was awash in green and blue shades, that Hope sat next to Phillip to speak with him.

"Good morning, sunshine," she said, rubbing his shoulder.

"Hello, dear." He looked up from his book about building structures around natural environments. "Is everything ok?" He couldn't help noticing that Hope was smiling at him rather largely.

"Yes…all is fine my dear…in the whole wide world, there could be no place as fine as this place during this time…and…" she paused.

"And…and exactly what?" Phillip noticed a splash of green light warmly tinting the left side of her face.

"Do you think that there is room here for another person?" she replied, looking down into her cup and back into his eyes.

"Another person?" Phillip tilted his head, trying to gather the clues, and in the early stained-glass light he noticed for just a moment, just a flash, a very bright candle burning within Hope's chest. As quickly as he spied it, it was gone. All of a sudden understanding came as he looked into her smiling face, her grin widening. "Another person... another person...my love, are you...are you?"

Hope nodded, "Yes, we are...we are going to have a baby."

Chapter 14

The
Burned-Out
Building

T he months flew by as Phillip and Hope both finished their classes, both graduating with honors within their fields of study, all this as they prepared their home for their little one. Dr. Jenkins was on standby as the days grew short and shorter, and finally the day of birth was upon them. Eric if it was a boy and Faith if it was a girl. This was a highly guarded secret that Phillip and Hope held for themselves, despite much prodding and requesting from friends. Such days are to be celebrated, to be joyfully absorbed into the marrow of breathing itself, but this day would hold in its hours a perfect balance of one life fading and another life unfolding.

Hope went into labor during the morning, when the hues of green and blues were cast across the wooden table from the rising sun. Dr. Jenkins knew right away that something was not right and went to work doing his very best with both lives in his hands. For hours Hope fought—she gave all that she was to bring the new unfolding life into the world. Fighting so that the new life would be able to see all the beauty and wonder and light that the world held, she fought for hours for their baby to come into the world to see and be a part of all of it. Phillip, beyond consolation, was pacing and searching within himself, sending pleas from the bottom of who he was out to the sky above, to the Candle Maker, to spare his wife and child. After an eternity of hours, the sun sinking to bed and deep rain clouds gathering, Dr. Jenkins came out of the door. Phillip knew instantly that something was wrong. In all his life he had never seen a tear in Dr. Jenkins eyes, and now there were tears and, far worse, pain.

"Phillip...I tried...I tried my best to save them."

The words played again and again throughout Phillip. Slowly they worked their way within his ears, deeper into his thoughts, yet deeper into his heart...the sharp, bursting, swelling words of loss, jamming and needling his inner workings apart. He felt as if a cold, unforgiving hand had reached within and was pulling away the better, far better, parts of himself....all that he was built of, all the beams being pulled apart, into helplessness, completely broken, beyond hurting, and all alone.

In a wounded, twisted pulse of energy, Phillip, shaking and sobbing, pushed past the midwife that was standing near him, out into the rain falling from a twilight sky that no longer seemed to care.

Phillip staggered through the wet, puddled, cobblestone streets of the Village for who knows how long. He wandered for hours in the pouring rain, walking without direction, without thought, without care, a husk of the person that just a sunrise ago was full of all things promising. Now, Phillip was empty.

His senses came to him, as he found himself sitting in a burned out building, the remnants of some old structure with most of the windows ruptured, beams charred from a long ago fire holding on defiantly against the weather and time that spilled freely here and there from the missing patches of ceiling overhead. The stone walls still held to a dream, a dream of what was, standing firm, perhaps waiting to be filled with people and light again. The rain worked itself in, steadily falling upon Phillip, a clump of clay hunched against a wall moaning out his exhaustion and pain.

To say that Phillip's candle flickered at this moment is truly an understatement. His flame, along with his heart, his life, his everything that Hope was to him, all of it, his entire pulse of existence, was just barely holding on. Like the last embers of a fire listening to the whispering secrets from the cold dark night that was closing in, approaching with its veil, nearer and nearer—he felt as if his light were giving itself over to the coldness of the night and the rain, almost as if it were spilling into the huge fault line that had opened up in the middle of his world.

The pitter-patting of drops mixed with his tears and heavy sobs. The weight of ache was suddenly broken by a voice and a light—a lantern, in fact— being carried by an older gentleman in an overcoat, hat, and umbrella, whose clear eyes defied his apparent age.

"Hello, you there! It's an awful night for sitting under the stars, especially when the stars don't even seem to be out." Testing the rain against his face, he looked out and up from under his tilted umbrella. "Some nights are colder, darker, and more damp that others…wouldn't you say, Phillip?"

Staring at the array of square stones that made up the floor, Phillip's voice, broken, empty of essence, thinly replied, "Do I know you?"

"In some ways yes, and in some ways no…no, you do not." Sitting near Phillip on an old, weathered wooden bench, he set the lantern down between them. "I was told to find you…to find you here."

The rain tarried on for long moments before Phillip, still gazing at the floor, noticing how the stones, because of age and weather, were uneven…faintly responded, "By whom?"

The older gentleman, watching ripples dance within the small puddles gathering around his feet, "By the Candle Maker….I was sent by the Candle Maker Phillip."

Phillip's head worked up to lean back against the wall behind him, rain trickling down his face and off of his chin. His face, like the stones around him, appeared carved, carved by a great pain, by a deep and inescapable ache eroding him as tears trickled and mixed in with the pouring rain. "Why?" Phillip half mumbled.

The older gentleman toying at a drip of water with the tips of his dress shoes, answered the question with a question: "Why was I sent…or why was Hope taken?" The words seemed to sift through Phillip like an open book of poetry.

"Why all of it…why any of it…why talk to you…why care for living anymore…why care for light…why care for a Candle Maker?" Phillip gave in response.

Sighing, the man peeked out at the sky from under the umbrella. "It truly is a cold and dreary night, Phillip", was his reply, and then, looking back at the tiny pools around his feet, he added, "no stars out at all."

There they both sat for some time until the older gentleman broke the falling sound of rain with his voice: "May I share something with you, Phillip?"

Phillip, mindlessly watched the visual race that droplet rivers held in streaks across a shattered, webbed pane of window. *Broken paths*, he thought, *rivers cut from running true*….He turned to the old man and spoke, his words hollow, "If you can offer any words that would ease me, please…please speak."

"This night is certainly a cold one, Phillip", he started, pushing off the bench and slowly bending to sit near Phillip, right upon the wet stones but holding the umbrella now so that it covered both of them, a lantern's worth of light between two souls in a fallen building. Phillip noticed the sound, the drumming of rain upon the fabric of the umbrella, a change in rhythm as the rain now was blanketed away from him.

"Phillip, we do not hold within us enough light to see all things that will come. We hold only enough to see through the course of a day and, if we are lucky, a bit at night under better weather than this. Just like this lantern here between us—it's not enough to shine open the darkness of this night, or even enough to illuminate what is left of this building, but here, here and now, between us—it's enough to see. I know that this doesn't work away what you feel, that which you are entitled to feel, but know that the road ahead, the road within and the road without, all of the long hard miles, the lows of valleys, and the peaks of splendid mountaintops, all are brilliantly lit by the love of the Candle Maker. We can barely see what's in front of us and even less make sense of it all, but know, Phillip, that the Candle Maker was there at your first step, at the very start of your journey, and through all of this, and…and the Candle Maker will be with you at your last step as well, at the very end of it all. The Candle Maker is there at each bookend of your life and all the pages between, shining."

Phillip slightly shifted his head to say, "If the Candle Maker is everywhere shining, shining like you speak of, why isn't he here? Why is my family gone…taken…ripped from me by this ugly, cruel life?"

A strange sparkling now lit in the older gentleman's eyes, defying the wrinkles that had been long worked into his face and the white hair sticking out from under his hat. "Hope is in good hands, Phillip, the best of hands, actually, but Faith…Faith is very much alive and well."

It took a moment to register, but it woke him from his fog. Rekindled and finding his way to his feet, strength building, tears now shifting to flow from a different part of his spirit, he burst out, "Faith…Faith…she's fine? She lives?"

The older gentleman, now standing as well, still holding the umbrella over them, placed his free hand upon Phillip's shoulder, eyes continuing to strangely sparkle, and through a weathered smile offered assurance: "Yes, Phillip, she lives. And you know what else, Phillip?" He looked around at the burned-out building housing them. "This place has potential; through the scars I can see something special here. I think there is life in these old bones yet. Well…I have got to go, places that I need to be, and come to think of it, I believe you have business to attend to as well. Faith is waiting for you…and, Phillip, one more thing—" he continued, his eyes focusing intently, "you will hold Hope in your arms again one day."

The older gentleman, with his umbrella, with a small gleam of lantern light, and with a certain grace, stepped over a blackened fallen pillar, out into the cold night, never to be seen again by Phillip, who in a pulse of straightened energy, was tearing away, splashing down the cobblestone streets toward home. The rain no longer fell, and a few stars began to appear in the clearing dawn sky.

Chapter 15

The Folded Paper

Upon entering the house, Phillip, soaked to the bone and dreadfully cold, walked up to Dr. Jenkins and hugged him firmly and spoke into his ear, "Thank you, my friend, for what you have given me. I am sorry I ran out without allowing you to explain completely. Thank you, my friend, for being here."

Dr. Jenkins held Phillip back at arm's length. "I tried, Phillip, to do all that I could to save them both...truly it was out of my hands...I have never seen a fighter such as Hope...she fought harder than I have ever seen to bring a new life into this world." Then he pulled Phillip back in close, this time speaking gently into his ear: "She wanted me to tell you that she loved you, Phillip, and that she knew the baby would be in good hands, the best of hands."

Crying the deep tears of joy, the new father asked, "Can I see her?"

Dr. Jenkins nodded several times. "Of course, Phillip. She is with the midwife."

He walked up to the midwife and smiled with gratitude and pride as she handed over tiny, fragile Faith, wrapped within a downy blanket, eyes opened looking out, a miracle gazing up at her father, a father gazing down into a miracle. Phillip felt the warmth of the fireplace, along with the warmth of overwhelming emotion.

Later that night as he sat gently rocking Faith in his arms, humming to her the soft melody of her mother's morning song, an idea began to stir within him. Words began to form, words from a sacred place within his heart, words that pleaded to be captured. He slowly stood, careful not to disturb the slumber of his little one, cradling her in his arms, stepping toward the desk, past a sleeping Dr. Jenkins, who had volunteered to stay in case further complications arose with the baby. With the preparations for Hope's burial in his mind, Phillip began to write, and out of him and onto paper these words were captured:

"The Candle Maker gifts a portion to us,
to each of us, a shimmering shard
of a much greater heart
placed lovingly within.
is it given for us to guard and protect,
or is it given to us to guide and direct?"

And at the bottom of the page he sketched out the silhouette of a human form with a small heart inside... above this a larger heart with lines of light cascading in all directions and also into the outlined body...this was his attempt to capture what he was feeling...to let the butterflies land on paper...to pull out of himself the idea of the Candle Maker placing a little bit of light, a small portion of a larger heart, a greater light, into each person. Questions accompanied that thought, as Phillip wondered, looking at what he had written and drawn: *Is such a gift given for each person to guard over, or is it more like a compass to guide the person from within, or maybe a bit of both?* He looked at Faith, who was asleep in a far land of perfect rest, dreaming within the slumber that only a new life can know. Phillip felt as if the words and drawing meant more than he knew, a part of a puzzle he was meant to hold onto. So he did just that, with one hand folding the paper in half and putting it inside the pages of one of Hope's books from the shelf, one of her favorites. He gently placed Faith down into her cradle, pulled a soft blanket over her, and walked to his bedroom door.

As quietly as he could he opened the door, lit a candle, and gently sat on the bed beside Hope. *She is as beautiful as ever,* he thought, noticing how her auburn hair lay upon and across the pillows. Phillip reached for her hand, and although it was cold, he felt the warmth of a life well lived and a death well given. He touched the silver ring on her finger and looked deeply at her face for a long time, knowing that he did not want to ever forget, even in death, how beautiful she looked. After a time he leaned in and kissed her upon her forehead and began to whisper to her, the words and tears falling upon her resting face: "I miss you terribly...I want you to know that my life is better because of you...so much better because I was able to be near you...I will watch over Faith, my love…I will do my best...I love you so much and you will always live within my heart…." and with one last kiss he stood, knowing that death's great divide now separated their bodies but not their spirits. He didn't look back as he closed the door behind him, for he had everything he needed to see, feel, and remember, right in the middle of his chest, right where the heart resides.

He reached over and rubbed Faith's cheek, humming Hope's morning song again without knowing it, lost in the admiration and splendor of a day that took so much and gave much more. He fell asleep on the floor right beside the cradle, lost in stained glass, morning songs, and trees falling in the forest to grow again.

Chapter 16
Stars Above

Faith grew—she grew more quickly than Phillip would have wanted, but such is the way with time, especially time spent within the peculiar and swift rays of parenthood. Enraptured by light, laughter, long walks along wooded paths, and discussions about the beauty within the world around them, both father and daughter grew into their new life.

Phillip found renewed breath by his position of leading a little light toward all things tremendous. He poured himself into project after project, all the while guiding Faith through the processes of writing, designing, building, and creating, patiently teaching her all the nuances of bringing things from the clay of mind to the life of reality. Phillip worked diligently on many great endeavors, including designing a covered bridge that gracefully spanned the widest part of the river near his village, a literature organization that brought together authors and poets from all around to work with one another and share ideas, and he played a great role in forming the first public library in the village, full of many books and adorned with artwork from local painters.

One project in particular captured Phillip's heart: the rebuilding of the burned-out building that he found himself in years ago. With help from close friends and many other great people who became friends, Phillip set to work rebuilding the roof, the walls, and the stained-glass windows, keeping the original heartbeat of the structure alive yet reinvigorated with new life. What was once a shell of a beautiful building held breath again; light poured through rich greens, bright blues, and sharp shades of yellow, spilling a rainbow upon the aged patterns of the stone floor.

Phillip didn't know why he was pulled so resolutely into the rebuilding of the charred remains, but something tugged at him night and day to bring the shine back into its arches. He found himself constantly thinking about the building and even dreamed of it often. Once he dreamed that he was sitting and watching the building from afar on a distant hilltop on a clear night with bright and beautiful stars overhead, listening to many people joyfully singing. From atop the hill, through the stained glass, he could see a massive amount of light pouring out in all shades of colors. He couldn't quite explain it to himself, the pull and hold that the building had on his heart and his deep desire to bring it back to life, but it beckoned to him and he followed.

Upon completion, Phillip began inviting people to the building for discussions upon matters of the heart, mind, and spirit, and before long a group of people formed weekly for meetings to share openly ideas of life and living with light. As news of such an open gathering of goodwill spread throughout the area, many new faces began to frequent the building, some being songwriters, some being musicians, others being excellent bakers and chefs bringing with them amazingly crafted cakes, soups, stews, and breads to share freely with others on any given night. It was because of this love that the building was suitably called "The Candle"—because it shone brightly as a center of welcoming and fellowship between all types of people searching for something better and brighter in the world around them.

One evening, after a few hours of laughter and conversations about the importance of graceful encounters and the uplifting of others, Phillip bid goodnight to the merry company and headed toward home. Outside, in the crisp evening air, a few steps away from "The Candle," he turned his head and heard the singing of many voices, the unified strumming of instruments, and from where he stood holding his daughter's hand, he saw a kaleidoscope of colors cascading out from the lungs of the building to breath into the dark night around them. He looked up into the stars above him and smiled. He looked down into the face of Faith and smiled even more.

PART
THREE

Chapter 17

All Things Great
and Powerful

Time's nature is that of moving, and in most instances, moving swiftly. Such it was with Phillip as time held him and his entire life in its current as it pulsed and pushed onward to eternity. In a blink, Phillip felt, so much time can pass, in the closing and opening of the eyes, so much can transpire.

In one moment Phillip felt as if he were looking down into the eyes of his little Faith outside the once burned-out building, and then he was looking into a great life that she had built for herself. Faith graduated from the University with exceptional marks in all areas and decided to dedicate herself to the pursuit of healing, working extensively with a retired Dr. Jenkins, who was now touched by age within his own river running its course, but alive plenty enough to share with Faith his life-long earnings of wisdom. Phillip was proud of Faith and all that she had accomplished: for her many accolades in the study of natural medicine, for her wit and charm, for her wide breadth of knowledge, and most of all, for her reputation of compassion that Phillip was sure was a trait she inherited from her mother.

It was through her many visits and constant letters that Phillip was introduced to Joshua, a fellow student devoted to the calling of caring for the sick and offering aid to those who need it most. Phillip was most surprised to find at his door one weekend evening Joshua knocking, discovering that he had made a special visit to speak with Phillip about taking Faith's hand in marriage.

Shortly after, Phillip proudly walked Faith down the aisle on a splendid spring midday ceremony, in which Dr. Jenkins presided over the ceremony as many people filled "The Candle" past capacity. Before Phillip was asked to give away his daughter's hand to a new life apart from him and his world, he looked up and noticed her profile as greenish blue light washed down from the stained glass to rest gently on her skin. He smiled, not daring to blink, wishing he could retain that image for all of ever, knowing that in her own way, Hope was present, a part of the joyous occasion.

Time carried onward, its currents rippling over, under, and through life as the unseen waters of sequence, and before Phillip could blink again he was pacing up and down the hall of the newly built house that belonged to Faith and Joshua as new life was being brought into the world.

Joshua sat with his leg jumping about frantically, chewing at his fingernails as Dr. Jenkins and his team of midwifes worked with Faith behind the doors of her room. Phillip paced back and forth for what seemed like infinite eternity, and then, in the blink of an eye, he heard the song of existence erupt, the wailing of a new life being forged into the world. Dr. Jenkins came out of the room, smiling from ear-to-ear and seeming younger than Phillip ever remembered. "She is here…and she is beautiful," he announced.

After Joshua visited with Faith, who although exhausted wished very much to speak with her father, Phillip was asked to visit privately with his daughter and granddaughter.

As if on holy ground, he walked into the room slowly and softly, unsure of what to say and how loud he should say it, feeling awed in the presence of such a sacred wonder. Faith disarmed him with a worn and tired smile, nonetheless full of light.

"What do you think, father?" The question came as she was looking down into the delicate life wrapped in downy blankets.

"I…I don't know exactly what to say, Faith…" looking at them both, "I…I am not sure the heart knows such a language to speak at moments like these." For just an instant, Phillip saw the light within his daughter, proud and glowing, and the soft steady flame of the small life she was holding dearly, just for an fleeting moment and it was gone. At this he began to cry, releasing the beautiful tears of joy, of ache, of triumph, and those from being in the presence of miracles. "Oh, Faith…my Faith…you have done good…so good…your mother is looking…looking down on all of us…and I know, Faith, that she is happy."

Faith began to cry as well, the tears of new life remembering the old, and the tears that come with holding a miracle within arms. "Father…I want you to hold her…here."

Phillip didn't know how to react at first, it had been so long, a blink of the eye and so much had passed, but he managed to reach out gingerly and receive the fragile little life. He held her softly and securely, as if it were the first and last life ever to be born. A feeling radiated up his arms and into his chest as he felt the warmth of all things great and powerful within the weight he held in his hands. Cradling her near to his heart, he asked, "So what will you name her?"

Faith smiled as she watched her father holding his granddaughter. "We have agreed to name her Hope… Hope, after my mother."

Chapter 18

The Final Speech

L ike a stone among the currents, life is run through the depths and along the sandy bottoms to become smooth and clean, polished and pure. Phillip saw many great things occur in "The Candle," many other weddings, jubilant festivals with food, laughter, dancing and music, and proclamations by many people of devotion to the Candle Maker, who made all things whole through love and light.

Phillip gave the eulogy at Dr. Jenkins funeral and other funerals of those close to him. More and more, as the river ran, people passed along and others were born. Phillip found more and more that many came for advice and to be encouraged, others sought insight into what a life was intended to be, and others had questions of light and the Candle Maker. With this, Phillip gave deeper portions of his energy, searching himself and leaning into the true nature of light. He began speaking and sharing to growing crowds that sometimes came two times in one day to hear him speak of and about the Candle Maker. It was given by many that Phillip held a strong connection to the Candle Maker, and as word traveled in wider circles, crowds began to pour into the once burned-out building to hear Phillip speak of a life under the guidance of true and brilliant light, the light that only the Candle Maker could offer.

It was on one day in particular, after a delightful morning visit with Faith, Joshua, and the just-learning-how-to-babble Hope, that he was making preparations to give a speech later that afternoon to a very large group that had gathered in "The Candle." Phillip, who usually prepared his thoughts by walking under the trees near the pond, had a difficult time finding the approach for this particular speech. He ventured back to his cottage to think, and while moving about a few books, he found that one had slipped onto the floor, one of Hope's favorites. The book was open on the floor, and by kneeling to pick it up, he found a folded paper that had slipped from within its pages. Phillip wept as he read the words, bringing back a night that laced its memory around his heart. He remembered his wife, he remembered her smile, and he heard her morning song; he remembered his mother, her care for him; he remembered Faith as a child, her little face looking up at him, her little hand within his; he thought of Hope growing again, a life from a life before, acorns into oaks, with new eyes and mind to witness the divine dance that is living...a garden of memory, a river of events and the course it had run. At that moment, he knew what he would speak about to the gathering crowd.

Later, as he stood in front of the crowd looking out into the mass of people, Phillip noticed how the stained glass danced brilliantly over the people sitting closest to the tall, arched windows. Phillip began to speak, the words seemingly taking a life of their own:

The Candle Maker gifts a portion to us, to each of us, a shimmering shard of a much greater heart placed lovingly within; is it given for us to guard and protect, or is it given to us to guide and direct? Either way, we each find that we, all of us, are pulled back to whence we came.

This light, this beautiful light within each of us, is tugging, reaching, growing back toward the light from which it was born. How powerful a candle's worth of flame, such power in something so small. Great and mighty oaks that live a thousand years began the size of an acorn—such power in something so small.

No matter how desperate and deep the darkness, the smallest flicker of flame holds mastery over it, igniting itself upon itself again and again, hope upon hope, over and over again, reaching to the far corners of the farthest caverns of our spirit—shining, standing, a beacon for all of us that we are more than we can ever know. We carry something beyond unique, beyond extraordinary—a testament scripted long ago that declares with all authority that darkness has no choice but to give way and bow before light, a light freely given, given to all, to each of us by the Candle Maker. A light to shine at our feet, to shine onto our path, through the thick expanses of a life, through the twisting vines of confusion and uncertainty, through the trenches of burden and toil, through the piercing thorns of heartache and pain—through all of these and more, light cuts the canopy to shine upon our faces. Light brings hope, dreams, and love, love that outweighs all and everything—the love of the Candle Maker.

There are those that would tell you that candles burning within you do not exist. To those my heart speaks: then why do we gaze into the distant diamond expanse at night and feel drawn toward it....Why do we marvel at sunlight as it washes through stained glass with its delicate strength to rest upon those around us?

There are those who would say that if the Candle Maker was real why isn't there proof....to those my heart speaks: in any act of compassion, of shared charity, an act of kindness to another in need, perhaps feeding the hungry or assisting those who struggle to provide for their families, and especially in the laughter of children….In these and in many more, there is not only the Candle Maker's face but the hands and voice also.

Worse yet are those who work against the Candle Maker, stepping in and out from shadows, putting plans into place in attempts to extinguish the candles within our fellow brothers and sisters. To those against the Candle Maker my heart speaks: you serve darkness and, as aforementioned, your fate is to tremble, broken and bowing before a light that is unbreakable.

So, what of our time, each of us, our allotment of days folding upon days, years upon years, our journey through this land and life together? After all, we are indeed pilgrims sharing a path….Let our time be invested within each other, into the growing of others around us, into outreach, into assisting, encouraging, and uplifting one another, let our tears be shared and also our laughter, let our hearts be rooted into the soil of all those around us, dividing the weight of existence together as we travel each step of our individual and collective journey.

So what of our words, syllable after syllable into the sentenced hymnals of all our breath given to speech? Let our words be one continuous song of love, of praise, a morning song to each we encounter, our breath given to work as wind lifting up others into each next unfolding moment….Also, let the words and songs of others be heard by you, one sweet choir, note after spoken note, melodies of compassion, like birds at sunrise celebrating the birth of another day, another chance to witness together the miracles that surround us.

So what of our actions, the hands of each moment digging, planting, harvesting? Let our actions have purpose, great purpose, substantial meaning, each an attempted masterpiece presented to the Master. With our actions, let us pull those who have fallen to their feet, let your works be the acorns of hope that will grow up and out of lives, let your actions outgrow and outlive you, reaching far to provide shade and comfort for those in generations to come, let our actions reflect the nature of the very light we have been given to carry.

The Candle Maker has given all of us a portion, a shimmering shard of a much greater heart. What each of you do with such a precious gift is ultimately up to you. Ignore it, try to diminish it, push away from it....Or perhaps you will accept it, allowing its warm glow to work through your time, your words, through the bridges you build out to others, through each moment and through each encounter. Maybe you will watch over and protect it from darkness that would try to blot out its flame. Maybe you will surrender to it and allow it to guide you through the vines, the mud, and the thorns. Maybe you will choose to search for it within yourself and also search for it within others.

All I know is that the gift has been given— how powerful a candle's worth of flame!

Phillip folded his papers into his hands and walked off the slightly raised platform toward his family, glancing down for a moment to notice his worn brown shoes stepping through shades of greens and blues, a river of stained glass washing his path toward a proudly smiling Faith and the outstretched arms of Hope.

Epilogue

The Candle Maker

After an excellent homemade dinner, conversation ripe with laughter, and reading Hope one of her favorite bedtime stories, Phillip bid goodnight to Joshua and kissed Faith on the forehead before heading back to his cottage. On the walk home he noticed how clear the autumn sky was and how bright the stars were as they danced in the heavens like sparkling crystals, pulsing in the vastness above to a rhythm he could barely imagine.

He sat on the edge of his bed after starting a fire in the hearth, which filled his cottage with cozy warmth, the sort of heat fit for sleeping. As the fire was snapping and popping, he looked up from his bed, noticing the wooden planks that patterned the ceiling, thinking about the vast puzzle of life and how each part seemed to fit together. He pondered all of the pieces: all of the places and people, all of the faces of loved ones, all of the songs and voices—from all he had lost, to all he had found, from all he had built, to all he had thought about—a life's worth of color, places, and shapes slowly turning over and over gently within his heart.

Phillip smiled as his body fell into sleep...his eyes closed, giving the body over to rest. His breathing became shallow and slowly edged into the currents and great understanding of the river of experience. Through the echo of a morning song he heard a voice...

"Phillip...my dear Phillip...awake."

Phillip's eyes lifted with the ease of youth. There was no weight to his head, no weight to his thoughts, no yield to his body as he lifted up, no aching, no touch of age, no breathing—none was needed. There, in a room that felt strangely welcoming even though he didn't fully recognize it, he saw all the gentle tools necessary for making candles, and there, at an intricately crafted wooden workstation, sat the Candle Maker, smiling, hands twirling and twisting about a piece of wax at the fingertips.

"It's you...oh my...it's you," Phillip spoke, feeling like crying more deeply than he had ever dared before, beautiful and painful crying that would shake all he was to the ground, but only one single tear formed.

The Candle Maker reached over and with a delicate hand wiped away Phillip's tear and spoke with the voice of heaven: "May I keep this?"

Phillip, surprised by such a sincere request, looked into the depths of the Candle Maker's face: "Yes….yes you may have it."

The Candle Maker's eyes embodied understanding. "Thank you, Phillip."

Phillip could feel the sensation of overpowering warmth course through him as he started to laugh. Then breaking into uncontrollable laughter, he felt as if he were surrendering to a musical joy that was shaking within him to release all the weights he had ever known and carried before, to which the Candle Maker began to smile and then broke out into wild laughter as well. Finally, both ebbing, quieting down, and each looking at each other like old friends reunited after years and years apart, Phillip felt the desire to speak but could not find appropriate words.

"What do I say?" exclaimed Phillip.

"You don't have to speak at all…or, if you choose, you can tell me some of it…or, if you wish Phillip, you may tell me all of it," responded the Candle Maker

Phillip moved his eyes across and around the room at the all the shapes, sizes, and colors of all the candles resting on shelves. Phillip noticed that some were long, some short, some wide, some thinner, some simple in appearance, and some intricately designed. He turned his gaze back toward the Candle Maker, who saw the questions in Phillips eyes.

"Each one different, but each the same," the voice sounding like midday spring, "each made to hold a share of my light."

The Candle Maker leaned closer, "By the way, don't you have something for me?"

Phillip noticed how silent it was in this workshop, more silent than he could compare to, like he imagined it sounded in the distance between stars.

"I have a candle inside me," Phillip responded.

"That you do, Phillip, that you do," the Candle Maker acknowledged with a smile.

"Am I supposed to give it to you?" Phillip asked, unsure if he asked the question by speaking or with his thoughts.

"Well, it has guided you here to me, and you have guarded over it very well....If you don't mind, Phillip...I would like for you to keep it."

At this Phillip noticed the light of a candle, a great greenish blue candle with three wicks that individually burned up and into one larger much brighter flame, burning within the Candle Maker's chest. Brighter and brighter, pulsing yet brighter until Phillip had to raise his arm to shield his eyes from the light, and then the candle softened, yet softer, ever so softly, back to before.

"You keep it, Phillip. It is the piece of me that I gave to you...the piece of me I wanted you to have all along."

Now Phillip heard singing, soft singing pulsing from outside the workshop. He recognized the melody at once. It was Hope's morning song, and it was growing louder, louder into a choir of voices.

Phillip looked toward the door. "May...May I... May I see?"

With an ocean of smiles the Candle Maker responded, "Yes, you may."

The Candle Maker turned toward the door and it slowly opened, allowing for a chorus of singing to spill through the opening into the workshop. Phillip found himself moving toward the door and out into the sweetest light, the greenest of greens, the bluest of blues, where he was greeted by a crowd of familiar faces: his mother, Dr. Jenkins, and his fair Hope singing the song he knew so well, her morning song, all of them with very bright candles warmly glowing from their chests, right where the heart resides.

Printed in the USA
CPSIA information can be obtained
at www.ICGtesting.com
JSHW082357140824
68134JS00020B/2128